MW01108280

Tales From
Dogman Country

Copyright © 2010 by Frank Holes, Jr.
All rights reserved.

ISBN: 1453762760
EAN13: 9781453762769

Tales From Dogman Country

Frank Holes, Jr.

To all of the Dogman fans in Michigan and abroad —

The Dogman is real.

Keep believing...

Also by Frank Holes, Jr.

Year of the Dogman

The Haunting of Sigma

Nagual: Dawn of the Dogmen

The Longquist Adventures: Western Odyssey

The Longquist Adventures: Viking Treasure

Acknowledgements Page/Disclaimer:

O NCE AGAIN, I humbly offer my work to you fans, based this time on both real stories I've collected over the years and my own imagination to fill in the soft spots. When actual sightings and encounters have been used, I've dutifully changed the names of the persons involved to protect the innocent (and perhaps not quite so innocent). And the stories of old, those great folktales, are indeed based on many real legends and myths from a great variety of sources around the Great Lakes.

As always, putting together a book for print requires the assistance of many people. My deepest thanks go out to the following professionals who have aided the success of this book: Craig Tollenaar, my awesome cover artist and illustrator, whose visuals absolutely captivate our fans and draw folks into the stories; Daniel A. Van Beek, who always stuns me with his attention to detail; Sergeant Todd Woods, Mackinaw City Police Department, for his help with the technical details regarding law enforcement; John Reick and the crew over at CreateSpace who have been such a pleasure to work with through all of my books; and Steve Cook, Traverse City DJ and creator of Stevie's favorite song "The Legend," which continues to be a great inspiration.

It is with great sadness that I am unable to credit Grandpa Eli here, as he was instrumental in inspiring me to write. He always read the first renditions and offered up his years of wisdom as only a grandfather can do. And he truly loved the Dogman stories, just as he'd always taught me to love myths and legends. It was very hard to see him go so suddenly. Grandpa Eli, you are missed greatly.

The collection of stories that follows is a work of fiction. Although the many villages, towns, and cities around Michigan are indeed real places, the story location itself exists completely in the mind of the author. Any resemblance between the folks who live there and people who live in the real world is coincidental and unintended. As for secret, undercover government agencies that sneak through the cracks of society, well, I'll leave that up to you fans to determine how plausible that one is.

The Dogman, however, is very real to those who have seen or encountered the beast. And believe me, I've collected dozens of stories from the good folks around Michigan. It's ironic that the best sightings and encounters come from people who never would have believed it before they saw it for themselves.

Official *Tales From Dogman Country* information and merchandise can be found at our website:

http://www.dogman07.com

Table of Contents

The Omeena Tale

1

The Pioneer Tale

15

The Tale of Claybank Lake

35

The Tale of Sigma

51

Markus's Blog

69

The Tale of Foster City

91

The Omeena Tale

The Omeena Tale

3387 B.C.

IT WAS DARK in the lodge as the old woman began her tale. Through the smoke opening at the lodge's ceiling, the six children gathered around could glimpse the last bit of purplish sky fading to black. The only light now came from the glowing embers of Wa-Kama's fire. Shadows danced upon the birch bark walls as the evening's last logs crumbled into golden and orange nuggets within the ring of smooth, charred river stones.

The story she would tell this evening was only for the children of the village who were nearing their own rites of adulthood. As the most venerated woman of the village, Wa-Kama was solely responsible for teaching the children of their history, their lineage. Even her name, Wa-Kama, meant both historian and storyteller, one of the most important roles in any tribe. Someday, she would choose her own replacement and pass along the Omeena tribe's full history, the long story of human existence. But this was only the first night of instruction, and she began not with the creation of the world, since every child had been taught that story early in life. Instead, Wa-Kama began with a far more intriguing tale, that of the downfall of their civilization, a tale from thousands of years in the past.

The four boys sat on the old woman's left side, near the fire for warmth because of their bare arms and legs. The two girls, both cloaked in the tribal women's traditional leather shroud, sat at Wa-Kama's right side. All of them perched upon Wa-Kama's many colorful woven blankets.

When she was sure that all the children were fully attentive, Wa-Kama began to speak slowly and with the passion of an expert storyteller.

"The Omeena, as you all know, are a proud people. We are an old people, tracing our line back to the ancients from the very first age of this world. Our tribe has survived even when others were left trapped in the past.

"The first age of this world was a time when the guardians, our own Nihuatl, still walked the earth. They were men, good and just, with the powerful magic to shapeshift into the mightiest creatures in our world—the great bears. In their animal form, they easily stood three times as tall as a man. They were like gods who would tread upon the earth. Their footsteps shook the ground. Even the largest trees in their path were easily broken to splinters. And they were guardians, protectors of our world, our civilization. They upheld the old traditions and the laws of the land.

"Most of the guardians wandered the vastness of our land, keeping the peace and the balance of nature. They traveled great distances, from the mighty glaciers in the north, to the mountains of the east, to the great sea in the west, and to the wide plains of the south."

The old woman was interrupted by a young girl whose long, dark hair had been braided tightly behind her head. Her dark, inquisitive eyes sparkled in the fire's glow. "Were the people afraid of the guardians, grandmother?"

Wa-Kama, who was reverently referred to as every child's grandmother, nodded her head. "In their Nihuatl form, the guardians were very frightening. And they could be unpredictable. The Nihuatl kept to themselves, and the people knew enough not to pursue them.

"Gera was the greatest of the Nihuatl warriors of the time, and second only to Nahma, their chief, in power and rank. Like the other guardians, Gera had lived for centuries, becoming more powerful as the magic of the natural world was absorbed by his Nihuatl body.

"But an evil sorcerer had poisoned the mind of the great Gera, filling him with pride and ambition. Gera had been convinced that he should lead the guardians, not old Nahma. Gera believed Nahma was set in his ways, that he couldn't see how the world was changing. Namha couldn't change with the world. The end of the second age of their world was coming quickly to a close; the second sun would give itself over to the third sun in only six more months. And if the end of the second age was anything like the end of the first, a great cataclysm was lying ahead of them. Their survival as a species demanded that the humans have the power to change with the world. Gera believed that he was acting on the civilization's behalf. He was convinced that he was the one to lead the humans into the third age of the world.

"On the eve of the summer's longest day, that holy day we call Nepessekee, the guardians met again in their sacred council glade. They had much to discuss. Messengers from the many villages had brought word of terrible events. Battles had erupted along the northern frontier, homes and farms were destroyed, and people from many tribes had been killed. Some even believed the Nagual, the evil skinwalkers, had found a way back to our world from the darkness beyond.

"Nahma, ever so difficult to persuade, discounted these stories. He wouldn't believe that the Nagual could have returned. The evil these demons had wrought in the first age of the world was the stuff of nightmares. It was far too horrific for him to imagine they could return. Besides, the guardians had banished the Nagual into the darkness at the end of the first age. Nahma believed there was no way they could have escaped from their prisons."

"But the messengers were right, weren't they?" interrupted a boy. He was sitting, cross-legged with his stone knife in his lap. He'd been carefully carving a set of arrowheads while listening to the story.

"Yes, you are right, my son," the old woman continued. "The Nagual had returned, and it was their evil that was causing havoc all across the land. These evil warriors, who looked like dogs and walked like men had been summoned by the blackest magic cast by the most powerful sorcerer of the age. He was called Xoloctal, and some believed he was a god cast out to live as a human on earth."

Two of the children shuddered, casting quick glances at each other.

"Yes, you've heard that name before," said Wa-Kama slowly, slightly raising herself to her knees. "It is the same name your mothers warn you about, the name they use to scare you. Xoloctal will spirit you away if you leave the safety of the village at night. Xoloctal will get you if you fight with your brothers or sisters or disobey your parents. It was Xoloctal who had poisoned Gera's mind, and yet he had never given away his true identity.

"At the council, the discussion soon became heated. Gera insisted that he be allowed to hunt down the Nagual and their sorcerer. His followers agreed heartily. Gera himself had seen firsthand the destruction of many villages. He had spoken with the few survivors. He knew the skinwalkers were moving through the land like a plague.

"Gera's outbursts at council were answered back by Nahma and his loyal guardians. There was not enough evidence to point to a supernatural cause. The many human tribes had been battling each other for territory and resources for centuries. There would always be disagreements between the people, often settled by violence. If the Nihuatl, led by Gera, got involved, there would be an outright war, one that would be devastating to the land.

"Nahma insisted that the tribes and their own local Nihuatl deal with the conflicts as they had for ages. He said that war must not erupt in the land."

Wa-Kama paused to answer a question from one boy. "Did every village have its own guardian?"

"Yes, my son," she answered. "The power of the Nihuatl is passed from generation to generation. These tribal warriors were not as large or powerful as the great guardians that met at the council glade. But they were the protectors of the local tribes, and they led their warriors in times of trouble."

"Do the Nihuatl always take the form of a bear?" asked the first boy with the arrow heads.

"Another good question, young man. The Nihuatl warriors can take many forms. The bear is the most powerful, but I also know of the jaguar, the eagle, the elk. There may even be other forms that men magically shapeshift into."

Wa-Kama resumed her tale, saying, "A fight for power arose when Gera insulted old Nahma and challenged him for leadership.

"Now, my darlings, Gera would have succeeded Nahma as the next chief guardian anyway. Nahma was old already, and huge and powerful though he was, he was weakening with each passing day. He hadn't hunted on his own for years, preferring instead to meditate in the sacred place and to teach the younger warriors. He was fed and groomed daily by his Tonal."

"What's a Tonal, grandmother?" asked another boy, enraptured by the story.

The old woman was pleased with the questions the children were asking. "Each guardian is linked spiritually with a Tonal, their human counterpart. Each Tonal acted like a priest and an advisor, and each used a variety of natural magical powers. These were different from the powers of the great Nihuatl. The Tonal could not shapeshift. Instead, the Tonal accompanied his Nihuatl, oftentimes riding upon the great animal's back. They worked together as the ultimate team."

Another question was posed by the first young girl. The second girl remained silent. "Grandmother, are there still Nihuatl and Tonals in our world?"

The old woman smiled gently. "You are already jumping to the end of my tale, darling. Wait until the story is finished and you will receive the answer.

"Gera was too greedy to wait for Nahma to pass along the leadership. Xoloctal, in his greatest disguise, had tricked the mighty hunter into issuing the challenge. Gera was younger and stronger than Nahma. But the old chief had lived a long, long time, and he was now more a creature of magic than he was ever a man."

"As the clouds massed in the heavens above and streaks of lightning lit up the sky, Gera charged across the council ring. He and Nahma were locked in a fierce battle. From the laws of the old traditions, no one else was allowed to interfere with a challenge of leadership, not even the Tonals. But it soon became too much for each of the combatant's loyal followers to sit idly by. Growls and snarls and the baring of teeth turned to skirmishes all around the council glade. Within seconds, every member of the council was battling. Even the Tonals, who had tried desperately to keep the peace, were now fighting alongside their Nihuatl. Magical spells ripped across the clearing, injuring the Tonals, though little damage was done against such powerful creatures as the other guardians.

"Nahma was holding his own against his adversary. The old chief didn't want to destroy Gera, but he did have to protect himself and his rank. Every slash of Gera's claws, every snap of his long teeth was redirected by Nahma. But what Nahma couldn't stop were the crushing body blows delivered by the younger guardian. Already the old chief could feel snapped bones within his own massive body."

"Couldn't Nahma have easily defeated Gera? He was the most powerful creature in the world, right?" asked the first boy.

Grandmother nodded. "The battle could have been over quickly if Nahma had used his own claws. But he refused to kill another guardian, even though Gera had been in the wrong. By constantly redirecting Gera's blows, the old chief was tiring out his younger adversary. The problem was, Nahma was tiring out, too.

"And that, my children, is when the unthinkable happened."

Every child's eyes were wide open and locked intently upon the ancient storyteller.

"All around the council glade, lightning began to strike the tallest of the fir trees. These great bolts of lightning were also joined by thousands of flaming arrows. Xoloctal's army had snuck into position and were now raining down a glowing curtain of fiery weapons.

"You see, my little ones, Xoloctal had tricked them all. He had played Gera against Nahma, and when all of the guardians were locked in a struggle to the death, Xoloctal set the trap.

"It had been a very dry summer season, and within seconds the forest was ablaze all around the council glade. With the exception of Nahma and Gera, the rest of the guardians had already been fighting to the death. A few had been killed already, and the rest were badly injured. There would be no escape for them from the blazing inferno.

"Nahma turned his head just for a moment to see the chaos that was completely obliterating his world, his life, his civilization. And that was when Gera struck. His claws slipped in past the old chief's defenses and slashed open a wide gash across the old bear's face. Nahma's right eye was gone in an instant, and the furred skin was peeled back from his ear to his snout. The chief's skull and teeth glistened in the firelight."

The boys all clenched their fists and ground their teeth in silent curses as the girls gasped, imagining the horrific sight of the gigantic, disfigured bear.

Leaning up over the children, Wa-Kama's passion matched the speed of her tale. "There was no holding back now. Nahma had to fight for his life. One eye was gone and the other was clouded by the dense smoke that was now filling the air of the glade. And still Gera continued the onslaught.

"The old bear ripped and clawed at the darkest of the shadows, sinking deeply into Gera's fur. And yet, despite the fire and the smoke and the battle wounds, Gera didn't halt for a moment. His mind had been so corrupted that he couldn't even see the devastation around him. His only focus was on destroying Nahma.

"Suddenly, the council glade was lit up as bright as day. A monstrous bolt of lightning struck, instantly killing two of the battling guardians. It was so bright that the bears' bones actually glowed right through their fur. Nahma was blinded, the color in his remaining eye drained to white, and his opponent had the advantage. Gera's claws tore chunks of flesh and fur from Nahma's body, and the great Nihuatl chief roared in pain.

"Still more lightning bolts crashed into the council glade, and soon the few surviving guardians ran for their lives, crashing through the burning trees all around them. Their fur caught fire and their eyes burned from charging through the flame and smoke.

"The Nagual were set loose to run the perimeter of the fire. These evil dog-soldiers caught anyone who managed to survive, even the Tonals, and ripped them to shreds. Even a few of the Nihuatl, the once proud and powerful guardians of the world, who had managed to escape the acres of blazing forest were no match for these evil predators who were awaiting them. Blinded, badly burned, and injured, the last of the Nihuatl were easy prey for the Nagual.

"In one bold attack, Xoloctal had defeated his greatest opponents, undoing them from within. The Nihuatl were no more. There was no longer any creature powerful enough to stop him from taking over the world.

"Finally, as the fingers of our holy sun began to creep over the horizon, the blessed rain poured forth from the heavens. The rain pelted the ground, hard and angry for days, and when the skies were finally empty, the barren land was a ghastly image of its once lush beauty.

"Our ancestors were left facing both the evil of Xoloctal and the Nagual, as well as the great cataclysm of the end of the second age of the world. And the once mighty guardians were gone. The human tribes were on their own."

Wa-Kama settled back on her blanket, spent from the tale. In her old age, it wasn't as easy to spin such a story, complete with the powerful emotions she had used to draw in the children.

"But what happened next?" the girl with the braided hair asked. "Our people survived. The evil was stopped. The sorcerer must have been defeated, or we wouldn't be here today."

The old grandmother smiled gently. In time, this girl, perhaps, might be trained as the next Wa-Kama. "You are as bright as you are beautiful, my daughter. But that story is best left for another night. Now, off to bed with you all."

And with that, the old woman kissed the young girl's forehead and then, despite their protests, she shooed the children out of the lodge.

It was a good story, Wa-Kama knew. It was one with a very surprising ending.

She used her walking stick to stir the embers of her fire. It was already cool outside, even as the summer days began to shorten. Now that the children were gone, the old woman carefully placed two logs on the coals to keep the lodge warm throughout the night. In just a few minutes, it was cozy inside again.

Yes, the girl had already surmised the ending, Wa-Kama knew, though not necessarily the details of the story itself. The Omeena had survived to this, the fourth age of the world, even though most of their fellow tribes lived on only in legends. The Omeena had been very fortunate indeed.

But evil still remained in the world. And good magic remained to combat it. As long as one existed, so too did the other to hold it in check. Wa-Kama knew, from the vast human history she retained in the deep recesses of her mind, that the Nagual would return yet again, always at the end of an age of the world.

And the dogmen would always bring death and cataclysm at that time if they were not stopped. When the humans were strong, when they were united, when they used their creative minds and skills, they survived to see the new age of the world.

When the humans were not strong enough, well, Wa-Kama knew their tribes wouldn't make it. She knew well that many tribes never made it to the beginning of the next age.

And when the humans couldn't stop the cataclysm, the devastation would be great indeed.

The Pioneer Tale

The Pioneer Tale

1877

DAVID MCMASTER SLOWLY scanned the edge of the dark forest for firewood. It was always his first chore after the wagons stopped each evening. Not that he didn't have other chores to do, too, but the fire was always of top importance. Without the fire, there would be no dinner. Without the fire, there would be no warmth. Without the fire, there would be no light.

Once it got dark here, far north of Lansing, it was nearly impossible to see. Dark here in the north was really dark.

The boy was hesitant to enter the forest. During their first two weeks, it was no big deal to gather downed limbs and sticks not too far from where they camped. They always stopped the wagons in a meadow or field just a little way off the trail, out of the way of any passersby. Though it was rare, occasionally a lone rider would come galloping down the primitive road. This happened mostly in the evenings, but the further north the pioneers traveled, the riders began to pass their camp later and later. David had no idea where these folks were heading. He couldn't even imagine anyone living in places further into the wilderness than they were now.

Traffic on the frontier during the day was nothing new. Riders traveled both south and north along the great trail, sometimes alone and other times in pairs or in groups of three. One time, the fathers had to pull their wagons completely to the side so that a coach pulled by a full team of horses could thunder past them.

But there were no settlements, no houses to pass. Only people on the move. And they never moved in the darkness.

Normally, David didn't mind his chores. It gave him a chance to see and explore a bit of the wild around them. This was going to be his new home, after all.

But tonight, something didn't quite feel right. It wasn't anything David could exactly put his finger upon, but the forest seemed spookier this evening. Darker and more sinister.

And their trail had been moving ever closer to the wooded areas all day. The fields were giving way to the dense forest.

Without thinking, his left hand reached into the pocket of his trousers and touched the sharp item he'd hidden there just this morning. It offered him no comfort, but still he wasn't going to just throw it away. There was something more to it. David didn't know what it was, only that he could feel its power, as if it were alive.

The boy could feel the hairs on the back of his neck prickle up. Goose pimples broke out on his arms, and he shivered despite the heat of the early summer evening. He looked out at the woods all around him uneasily.

It was as if the forest had eyes looking back at him.

David scooped up the load of firewood he had collected, not even an armful, and ran back to the camp as fast as his legs would take him. In his mind's eye, he could see some sort of large, dark creature already stalking after him.

* * *

They were now three days north of the village of Greenville. It had been the last vestige of civilization before the final push to reach their destination. While their livestock rested, David and his father had walked into the village to restock their supplies. At that point, they were a little more than halfway through their long journey. They could fully load the wagons again and still have some supplies on hand as they made their new home in the village of Evart.

Two to three hard weeks of travel still awaited them. The trail north from Greenville was not nearly as well maintained as the track they'd taken northwest from Lansing on the first leg of their journey. That was an actual road. It was dirt and bumpy, but the stumps and rocks had been hauled out years earlier.

Just one day out of Greenville, the trail was nearly gone from sight. Only the matted grasses and faint wagon ruts gave them the notion that they were traveling in the right direction. And occasionally a traveler would pass them, tipping his hat to them in greeting before moving on his way.

And this trail was rugged. The wagon bounced so much that the families preferred to walk alongside their teams of oxen rather than ride. Neither family owned a horse, but they each had a milking cow tethered to the back of their wagons. It wasn't too difficult to maintain a nice walking pace and still keep up with the animals.

The trail led fairly straight north through the mixture of grassland and forest. Sometimes the woods were dark with thick pines, the sunlight having difficulty penetrating through to the needle-covered ground. And other times it opened up more into groves of massive oaks, aspen and birch. These groves were most difficult because of the substantial undergrowth that hid logs, stumps, and large rocks from view. About once a day, the members of both families would have to roll up their sleeves and disentangle the lead wagon from whatever obstacle it had encountered.

But ahead, everyone could see the dark green band of forest that stretched across the horizon. Ahead, they all knew, the grasslands would cease and their path would lead them fully into the northern Michigan wilderness.

* * *

The McMaster family and the Smith family, neighbors in the capital city of Lansing, sold everything in the spring of 1877, lock, stock, and barrel. The families' fathers, James McMaster and Theodore Smith, worked together at the Biddle Bank and Trust and were long time friends.

The great change in their lives came when Smith's younger brother, Alexander, sought his fortune in the north. He was one of the first to establish a lucrative lumber mill in the tiny village of Evart. Located right on the banks of the Muskegon River, Smith's mill had become a major player in the lumber industry in just a few short years. He was in need of businessmen with banking experience to grow both the mill and the village into what he described as the "Land of Green Gold."

In a letter to his brother Theodore in the fall of 1876, Alexander promised the deed to 40 acres outside the village of Evart to any businessmen willing to take on this extraordinary adventure. This was in addition to all materials necessary for the building of a first-rate residence and a fine annual salary working at the mill. Of course, Alexander had hoped it would be his brother who would take him up on the offer.

A week's time was all it took for James and Theodore to agree to convince their families. The two children were excited, and David, James's son who had just turned 11, thought it was the greatest adventure a boy could have. On the other hand, Abigail, Theodore's 10-year-old daughter, was always nervous when David began talking about Indians and bears and wolves. She wasn't so sure about moving into the wilderness.

Alexander had said it was a 120-mile trip, but how long it took depended upon the weather. As soon as the snow melted, the families sold their homes and most of their belongings. They each purchased a wagon, complete with the tall hoops that held up the canvas coverings, as well as a team of oxen to pull it. Supplies for the trip took up the most space, and there was little room for personal belongings. They had to take everything they'd need, not only for the trip but also to establish their homestead. It would be hard telling when they'd have a chance to resupply themselves.

At night they slept beneath the wagon or under a lean-to tent, depending on the weather. They cooked simple meals over an open flame in cast iron pans.

And they stayed close to each other for safety. You just never knew what might be lurking in the darkness.

* * *

The day after leaving Greenville, a lone rider joined their wagon train in the late afternoon. He was a trapper by trade, heading northwest to Grand Traverse City, the largest settlement in the far reaches of the Michigan woods. Of course, David's family was more than pleased to share their camp and fire with the man who called himself "Black Jack."

Their guest was a stout fellow whose skin was tanned and a bit weather-worn. His long, dark hair had been pulled back and tucked behind a gray, furred hat. Above his wispy beard, Black Jack's dark mustache curled upwards at the ends, nearly touching his wide nose. Hanging around his neck and over his faded leather vest was an array of pouches of various sizes that held items he might need at a moment's notice.

As was customary going back to ancient times, a traveler repaid the hospitality of his hosts by sharing news and stories.

Once their dinner of stew and biscuits was over and the meal completely cleaned up, the adults took their thick coffee and settled around the fire. They laughed and sang the old church songs, and Abigail's father played his harmonica. David's father read them a chapter from the Bible (the only book they'd brought with them from Lansing), and by that time the two kids were quiet and respectfully listening as Black Jack began sharing news from the frontier.

He answered questions about his life and career from the adults, telling them about the many little settlements that were springing up all over the north. Pioneers from Lansing, Battle Creek, and Saginaw were establishing footholds over the wilderness. Lumber mills dotted the forests, and some of the mighty trees ol' Black Jack had seen were wider around than their covered wagon was tall. These great logs were floated down the land's rushing rivers to the cities, where manufacturers produced the materials that built the homes and businesses in our state.

"I've even seen huge sailing vessels upon the Great Lakes," Black Jack told them. "In my time traveling through Fort Mackinac, Fort Gratiot, and everywhere between the seaside ports of Pere Marquette and Alpena, mind ya, I've watched as settlers flock like birds upon the growing cities of the north. It won't be many years, my good friends, before the wilderness is opened wide to railroads and the comforts of true civilization.

"The settlements themselves were growing, too. The little lumber camps were quickly becoming towns. Trade was opening up as the trails between towns and villages became more widely used. And folks had pretty good relations with the local native tribes."

"Tell us about the Indians," David insisted despite a sideways glance from his mother. Both of the mothers had been knitting by the firelight, a practical and entertaining pastime. But neither was very keen on listening to stories of the wild. They only did it out of respect for the old customs.

Black Jack gave them a wide grin across the campfire. Abigail thought it creepy because there were two gaps where teeth were missing. Since he'd removed his cap, the fur trapper's long, unkempt hair also wiggled in the slight breeze, adding to his wild appearance.

"Well now, my lad, there are three main tribes living in the wild," began Black Jack, tamping a pinch of tobacco into his long pipe. "There's the Ottawa and the Chippewa in the north, and the Potawatomi who live mainly in southern Michigan. They're a pretty good bunch, that they are. Wise in the ways of the land. Not met a one I didn't like, no sir."

"You've spent considerable time with them?" asked Abigail's father.

"Oh, yes," Black Jack answered. He blew out a nearly perfect smoke ring that floated up over their heads and off into the darkness. "Oftentimes, I work right alongside many of them. Indians always seem to know the best places to trap. And they have great ways of skinning and preserving the furs so they reach as far as Lansing and Jackson in tip-top shape."

"If you don't mind my asking," David's father posed, "is the fur business fairly lucrative?"

Black Jack gave them all another wide grin. "Oh, yes, my friends. And business is good. Folks with money, especially the ladies, like to dress up in grand fashion with beautiful furs. I take orders in the cities and then head north to load 'em up all winter long. I can probably make a dozen trips back and forth each year, depending on the weather."

"So the Indians aren't savages, then?" asked David, sounding disappointed.

"No, my lad," answered the trapper, chewing on the end of his pipe. "They might have been fierce in the past. But as far as I can tell, the only thing savage about 'em now is their stories. And let me tell you, they've got some good 'uns."

"Tell us one of their stories, please?" David begged. Again, his mother shot him a dark look from above her knitting pins.

"Well now," began Black Jack, "I 'spose I can do that. Both the Ottawa and the Chippewa share a story that's not too unlike an old French legend I grew up learning from my own Granpere. It's a deep, dark legend about a creature that is believed to haunt the woods at night. My Granpere called it the *loup-garou*, the 'man-wolf,' a creature that looks like a wolf and walks like a man. The Ottawa called it the *wiindigoo*, an evil spirit that takes the physical form of a man-like beast that craves human flesh. They're well known, by the Indian tales that is, to even sneak into villages at night and carry victims away."

Abigail shuddered, snuggling in closer to her father. Being a banker by trade, he only smiled and put his arm around her. He believed in the reality of numbers and ledgers, and stories were just fiction to him.

Black Jack continued his tale. "This *wiindigoo* sometimes possessed an evil man's soul, and if the man possessed enough *Mide*, that's a spiritual magic they believe in, mind ya, he could even change his shape. Yes indeed, lad. That evil man became one with his animal totem, becoming, in this case, a wolf that walked like a man."

"So did these *loup-garous* hunt people?" David asked, fascinated.

"Oh, they were plenty terrible," the trapper said. "I was even afraid myself many nights, when I stayed alone in the wild lands. The *loup-garou* is often said to search out and devour those who leave the safety of their villages. And there's nothing that can stop them."

"But it's just a story, right?" squeaked Abigail.

"Here, look at this beauty, and then you decide," Black Jack said, reaching into the deep satchel that slung around his neck and shoulder. In the glow of the campfire, everyone could see the long, curved claw he held up. Handing it to David's father, Black Jack said, "Be very careful, it's still very sharp."

The two fathers each took long glances at the black claw. Abigail and the two mothers declined. Finally it was David's turn. He turned it over and over in his fingers before finally handing it back to the trapper.

"Where did you get it?" the boy asked excitedly.

"Ah, you like that, do you? An Ottawa man named Croton, one I would consider my friend, not too far from this area in fact, traded it to me, a few years ago. We often trapped along the Muskegon River together. He believed the claw belonged to a *wiindigoo*, and it held some sort of great power, but he was unable to just discard it. It wouldn't let him, he told me. But when he traded it to me, he said he felt relieved. He said the claw was ready for a new master.

"And then a year later, I'd returned to that part of the state to trap with Croton again, but the villagers said that he'd died. They believed he had been killed by the *wiindigoo*. Well, I haven't gone back to trap the Muskegon River anywhere near there since then. It might be a bit more traveling for me to avoid the area, but I believe there's something to that old legend. Something sinister, something real."

A muffled whimper was heard as Abigail cried against her father's woolen shirt.

"I think the children have had enough of the tales for one night," Abigail's mother said, giving Black Jack a slight scowl and shooing the kids toward the tents. "Off to bed with you two." David's mother led the way.

As he headed toward his family's lean-to tent, David heard Black Jack apologize to the fathers. "I didn't mean any harm," he said regretfully.

"You are fine, my friend," Abigail's father replied. "The women are skittish already about being so far in the wilderness. You know how they get anyway. And such stories are always better among the men. Besides, now we can share a little nip of whisky before we turn in."

"Oh, ho, I like that. A most excellent idea, my friend, most excellent indeed. And how about another tale or two?" It was the last of the conversation David heard before crawling into his sleeping roll.

* * *

Black Jack and his painted horse were long gone by the time the members of the two families awoke. They hadn't expected anything different; travelers along the trail sometimes had to make long journeys while the light lasted, and everyone went his own way. Black Jack must have had many, many miles to go before sundown.

David's mother stirred up the coals from the night before, quickly igniting a few smaller dry sticks for the breakfast fire. It would be just enough to boil up a pot of coffee and fry up a few johnnycakes for everyone. While the women cooked, the men and kids broke camp.

David was just adding a pair of larger sticks to the fire when something in the pile caught his eye. His clever fingers reached downward and brought up Black Jack's claw, the one he'd shown them the night before.

He must have dropped it here, David thought innocently. Quickly, before his mother could turn around and see, he stuffed it into the pocket of his trousers. It wouldn't do to have her see it; she'd undoubtedly make him throw it off into the woods.

David kept it safe in his pocket, a secret he didn't share until they stopped again a few nights later.

* * *

"Abigail, come look at what I found," David said beckoning her closer. With the dense forest all around them, they'd both been sent to gather wood, and water, together for safety. Abigail was about to fill the metal pail from a rippling creek when David pulled the claw out of his pocket and held it up for her.

"Ugh, that's that thing the trapper showed us the other night. How did you get it?" she asked, setting down the half-filled bucket.

"I found it by the fire the morning he left. He must have accidentally left it behind. Maybe dropped it."

"You sure you didn't just sneak it away from him, David McMaster?" Abigail asked, squinting her eyes and trying her best to imitate her mother. She wasn't too far off the mark.

David frowned. "No, I didn't steal it. I found it right in the pile of firewood. It's too nice to just leave behind. Maybe I'll make a necklace out of it."

The little girl stared at him, her hands on her hips. "Your mother is going to stripe you good if she catches you with it. Besides, it's scary. You've been having nightmares, haven't you? Don't deny it, I heard you in your sleep."

David didn't want to admit that in the two nights he'd possessed the claw, he'd had two of the worst sets of nightmares he'd ever had in his life. Since the members of both families slept within yards of each other, everyone else would have known if he'd cried out in his sleep.

When he didn't answer, Abigail started in on him again. "You've had that claw two nights now? And you've had nightmares both nights. That's a coincidence, don't you think?"

"I don't know," David answered angrily. "I shouldn't have shown it to you in the first place. You're a girl, you wouldn't understand."

Now it was Abigail's turn to be put out. She was about to scold him again when they were both startled by a noise from the woods ahead of them.

The two of them were rooted to the spot, unable to turn and flee. In moments, they began to hear something moving through the brush, coming toward them. It growled with each step.

David's father had instructed him to try and scare off any large creatures they might encounter in the forest, whether they were boars, wolves, or even bears. *They're likely more frightened of you than you are of them,* his father had told him. *If something gets too close to you, and you can't get help, try to scare it away. Act big and tough, and throw something at it if you can. That'll help.*

Remembering his father's advice, David hollered at whatever was pushing its way toward them. "Go away! Go away!"

And then the creature was before them, standing on all fours about 25 feet away across the creek. David assumed it was a wolf, even though he'd never seen a real one in his life. It matched his father's description. But it was so huge! He could hardly imagine that a wolf could be so big. It easily equaled the boy in height, shoulder to shoulder, head to head.

David shouted once again, and this time he threw a large stick from the bundle across the creek at the creature.

It was a good throw, and it should have hit the creature right across the bridge of its snout. However, in a bold move, the creature's left paw shot up and actually caught the stick right out of the air.

And then, to both children's surprise, the creature stood up on its back legs and stared down at them from the opposite bank. Even without the added height of the embankment, the monster stood twice as tall as Abigail.

In a quick flick of its paw (which David could now see was made up of fingers, just like a human hand), the beast snapped the stick in two.

"I think it's that *wiindigoo*," David whispered. Abigail was far too frightened to speak, to nod, or even to breathe.

With a powerful grace, the beast stalked forward on its hind legs, slowly one step at a time until it reached the water's edge. It was only about 15 feet away now, and it squinted up its eyes and snout to growl at the two kids.

"I think you should give it your claw," Abigail startled her friend by finally whispering back. "Remember what Black Jack said about his Indian friend? That claw belongs to it."

"No way," David hissed back. "It's mine. I found it, I'm keeping it."

The creature curled up its lips again and this time bared its long, sharp teeth. A deep growl emanated from its throat, much louder than the first time.

Suddenly, with a stroke of speed David didn't know she had, Abigail snatched the claw from the boy's fingers. The skin on both of their hands was cut in the process from the sharp edge of the claw. Before David knew what happened, Abigail threw the claw across the creek toward the monster.

Completely mesmerized by the beast, David didn't have time to be angry with Abigail. Nimbly and gracefully, the monster reached out one long, hairy arm and snatched the claw out of midair.

But the two children were still far too scared to run. They stood, motionless next to each other staring at the creature across from them. Slowly, Abigail slipped her left hand into David's right. Then she cautiously began to pull him back away from the creek, one careful step at a time.

The beast, on the other hand was examining the treasure it had reclaimed. It wasn't paying any attention to the children.

If we can only get out of sight, Abigail thought, *maybe we can sprint back to camp. Or at least hide somewhere until it goes away.*

However, just as they were nearly concealed by the undergrowth at the creek's bank, David stepped on a twig. Its loud crack pulled the beast's gaze away from the claw. Immediately, the creature snapped its head up and glared at the two children.

Abigail froze again, squeezing her fingernails into David's hand. The monster bared its fangs at them and let out a menacing snarl.

Petrified by the creature's glowing eyes, the two children were completely unprepared for it to suddenly spring all the way across the creek. The beast landed close enough for each of the two kids to reach out and touch its dark, matted fur.

David had just enough time to shut his eyes and tuck his head down, expecting the very worst.

And then, the beast was gone.

The boy slowly peeked out at the world, but the only thing there was Abigail.

"It jumped right over us," she said blankly, obviously in shock. "I watched it. The whole thing. It happened so fast."

"Are you sure we're not dead?" David asked slowly.

Abigail thought for a minute, trying to make up her mind. "No, we're still here. But I feel sick. I think we should get back to camp, right away David. You might have to help me."

And with that, the girl passed out, falling forward onto David's chest. He caught her and held her closely for a few minutes, hoping she'd wake up. He could hear her breathing so he knew she was okay. But she needed help. That thought finally got him going. He scooped her up and, though it was a bit of a struggle through the forest, carried her back to camp.

As the white of the wagons' canvas came into view, David turned and risked one last look back into the thick forest. He thought he saw a pair of glowing yellow dots in the darkness. They didn't move. They didn't blink.

Quickly, the boy hustled as fast as he could back to camp. That encounter was far more perilous than any he'd ever wanted on their journey.

The Tale of Claybank Lake

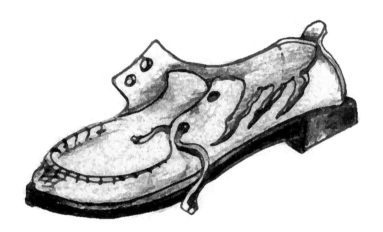

The Tale of Claybank Lake

1967

SHERIFF MANNY BLODGETT sat uneasily at his desk. The old chair squeaked every time he leaned forward or reached back to scratch his butt. The heavy swivel chair had been in the Manistee County Sheriff's office well beyond the 22 years that Manny had been employed there. When he took over as the boss 10 years earlier, he'd learned that the old chair predated even Sheriff Cooper, who'd sat on the throne for nearly 30 years himself.

Manny always guessed it dated back to some old World War I manufacturing hub someplace in the Midwest. Considering the chair's size and the thickness of the steel holding it together, it had to have been made in a time when the world wasn't disposable. He himself started his career in the midst of America's Golden Age of Capitalism. In his time, Americans had become real consumers, buying more and more things to fill their houses and garages in the suburbs. At the same time, eating TV dinners, using disposable razors, and drinking from Styrofoam cups became the norm, as advertisers urged Americans to buy more and more disposable products.

And then the world began to see *slippage*, as Sheriff Manny always saw it. When the quality of a product began to decline, when it didn't last as long as it should have, when it broke under normal conditions of use, well, Manny believed that was slippage. *The whole world is facing slippage*, he often told himself. It wasn't just the products that were manufactured. You could see slippage in people, too. In his job, he often did.

The old chair, on the other hand, it was designed to last. Manny was pretty sure it was already over 50 years old, a throwback to a time when products were made to last dang near forever. He often guessed it would still be here in this office, doing its duty as it was meant to, for many more sheriffs to come.

This evening, the chair was making quite a bit of noise. It was nothing that a couple of sprays of WD-40 couldn't fix, but Manny had little time for that. He was still going over the latest report, rereading it line by line, trying to make any sense of it all.

* * *

The sheriff's patrol had been called in by a neighbor, a Mr. James Bowden. The call came in at 2:40 pm on Saturday, April 1. Dispatch originally thought it was an April Fool's Day prank, but it was passed along to a patrol, who found out it was no joke.

Officers arrived at the scene, a dirt road leading to a cottage just up from Claybank Lake off of Carlstrom Road. It wasn't right on the water, but it was fairly close.

The neighbor met the two deputies there. The ground was still covered with a few inches of snow, and the larger drifts could be seen beneath the stand of pines nearby. It had been a very harsh winter, one which refused to let its grip go, even here in the first week of April.

One deputy began questioning Bowden while the other tried the front door.

James Bowden, according to the report, was a friend of the victim. Or at least the closest thing to a friend that Terry Dellis had. Since Dellis was homebound (and a recluse by nature), Bowden often brought him groceries and any mail, usually every two or three weeks. The last time he'd checked on Dellis was on March 14 when he'd dropped off, among other things, beer and olives for St. Patrick's Day. Dellis was an old Greek, Bowden noted, and though he disdained American olives for lacking size and flavor, they were still the only olives he could get. St. Patrick's Day, though not important to a man of Greek descent, gave him an excuse to drink a lot of beer. Bowden said that he'd bring the largest jar of olives he could buy at Oleson's Market on every trip, and in the trash he'd undoubtedly see the empty jar from the previous visit. Bowden also apparently took Dellis's garbage to the city dump and dropped his bills off at the post office on these visits.

Bowden had arrived just before 2:30 and found the front door locked. Normally Dellis left the door unlocked for him, so this immediately raised concern. Of course, looking through the window and seeing the victim's upside down body protruding through the floorboards prompted Bowden to drive home immediately and call the sheriff's office.

During the interview with Bowden, the second deputy was totally perplexed. The front door had still been locked. In fact, the snow had drifted up onto all sides of the cabin. The only tracks in were those of the neighbor. Finding probable cause (he could see the body inside as well), the deputy forced open the front door. There was no smell from the body because the house and its contents were pretty much frozen solid.

Here, Sheriff Manny stopped reading and instead thought back to the conversation he'd had with Ben Cunningham, his longtime deputy, the one who'd first stepped into the victim's residence. Reading the report just didn't do Ben justice; the whole description was better off told in Ben's own words.

* * *

"I'm a-tellin' ya, sir, that fat porker was just a-pokin' up outta the floor like a lawn dart," Ben started out in the southern twang that hadn't left his voice in 20 or more years. "It was pretty gruesome, that's fer sure. There were frozen trails of dark blood comin' down the stumps o' his legs and it stained his blue jeans and the floorboards. One look was more than enough for me."

The sheriff had indeed seen some gruesome sights in his years in law enforcement. The worst always seemed to be in traffic accidents, but every once in a while something from the normal side of life caught you unexpectedly.

Deputy Cunningham continued his tale. "After a few minutes tryin' not to lose m' lunch, I fine'ly got up enough nerve to give him a few pokes, you know, to see how long he'd been there. Well, sir, he was a reg'lar popsicle, if you follow me. Frozen stiff. And as hard as a chunk of cement." This last word came out sounding like "see-ment" and Manny worked hard at keeping a straight face. Listening to Ben always made him want to smile.

"He 'bout as heavy, too, I reckon. I sure am glad the meat wagon guys got t'extract him. I'm sure it woulda thrown my back out. But the strangest thing," Ben went on, "was the hole in the roof. Sun was a-shinin' right through, sir. There was even a build up of snow inside the cottage."

"Any ideas what might have caused it?" Manny remembered asking.

"No clue," the deputy answered. "If a tree had fallen on the house, it woulda still been there. Shoot, if some part of a NASA rocket had fallen right outta the sky and crashed through the roof, there woulda been shrapnel ever'where. Now, I gotta tell ya, there was a buncha splinterin' from where the loft gave way, and a-course where the vic crashed through the floor. But sir, the inside o' that place was just as normal as normal gets. I didn't see anything unusual."

* * *

The two deputies sent Bowden on his way. He was as local as you could get, and after such a shake up in his normal boring afternoon schedule, he wasn't going anywhere anyway. They could find him for more questioning if that ever became necessary. However, neither of the two officers thought they'd need to.

After calling for the ambulance and coroner, the two deputies cordoned off the cottage and made their official sweep both outside and inside.

There was no sign of forced entry. The windows were still intact. The only breaches in the cabin were the hole in the floor which was plugged by the body and the hole in the roof which was still wide open to Mother Nature.

Had it been foul play? The weather would have erased any trace of tracks from people or vehicles. Had it simply been an accident? There was nothing anywhere to explain the hole in the roof.

The scene inside the cottage gave an equal lack of explanation. There was a huge dead guy stuck upside down in the floorboards all the way to the fat rolls at his waist. His feet were gone. It wasn't that they were missing; they were completely gone. All the deputies could find was a pair of shredded leather moccasins across the room. The feet were never found.

Up above the dead man, there was a hole in the cottage's loft where the floor above apparently had given way. The boards and beams making up the simple joist system had snapped and were either hanging down by their last strands or smashed to splinters all around the victim.

* * *

The next part of the report had been typed up by the county detective, Dave Ashley. Dave wasn't a full-time employee of Manistee County, but shared by the law enforcement departments in nearby Benzie County and Leelanau County on an as-needed basis. Again, Sheriff Manny found his report about as interesting as watching the Laurence Welk Show. It gave great insight into the events that befell Terry Dellis, but there was still something missing. Something HUGE was missing—the cause of it all.

Manny's mother used to say "the devil's in the details." This report was as full of details as it was full of devils. The problem, as the sheriff saw it, was that the details didn't connect to a larger picture. These devils only mocked Sheriff Manny because they knew what caused the whole thing to happen in the first place. But those devils refused to tell the whole story.

Dave's investigation didn't take long. The unstable flooring system in the loft was caused by a ceiling leak. The little rivulets of ice gave it all away. Water had backed up under the shingles and dripped onto the loft, Dave guessed, for more than 10 years. He'd even found a mop bucket buried and smashed in the rubble. As Dave saw it, the deceased had probably used it regularly over his early years, though he never fixed the roof. However, as Dellis became far too obese to travel up to the loft—Dave's best guess was that no one had been up there for a long, long time because of the heavy layer of dust, cobwebs, and the collection of odds and ends that would otherwise have taken up space in a home's attic—the bucket just filled up without ever being emptied. Every drip from the roof eventually ended up on the loft floor, slowly compromising its integrity.

However, Dave believed Dellis had gone into the loft just moments before the episode happened. Something had triggered him to head up there. The wooden step-ladder had been pulled up onto the loft, and one of the rungs was nearly cracked in half. Dave believed it had been damaged by the heavy weight of the victim as he had climbed upward.

Terry Dellis's weight was far too much for the rotten floorboards. The loft would have given in with a loud, continuous series of snapping boards, kind of like machine-gun fire. Like a sinker at the end of a fishing line, Terry's heavy frame would have dropped through the opening, giving him no opportunity to even flail his arms for balance or reach out for purchase. In the fall, his body turned upside down and he crashed headfirst into the floorboards below. Because these boards had also been slowly damaged by water for many years, seeping down from above, their rotted sections easily gave way to the man's bulk.

His head and shoulders burst through into the cabin's crawlspace, but there Terry's body stuck fast. His flabby arms were pinned tightly between his barrel chest and the thick floorboard sections that had not broken upon impact. From that distance, his head would have still been a few feet above the frozen ground in the crawl space. The man could have kicked and screamed and struggled, but the more he wiggled the more stuck he became.

As for the hole in the roof, Dave Ashley had no idea. Of course, Manny had verbally beaten him up for his lack of opinion, but Dave refused to speculate. There simply was no evidence to explain it. He wouldn't go out on a limb with a guess because there was no limb to climb out on. It was unexplainable.

* * *

Manny rubbed his temples with his wide right hand. The old office chair continued its squeaky chatter as the big sheriff shifted his weight for the umpteenth time that evening.

The conversation Manny had had with the county coroner weighed heavily on his mind. Instead of tying the puzzle together, it only raised more questions. They'd met at the morgue that next morning, talking over the huge, covered body of the late Terry Dellis.

"He weighed in at 407 pounds," the coroner said. He breathed out a sigh just recalling their afternoon's workout. "It took both of the ambulance boys and myself to pull him outta the floor. And he was frozen solid. That cottage, with no heat for several weeks, acted just like a freezer. Sheriff, surely you remember some of those frigid days we've had."

Manny nodded. There hadn't been a ton of snow accumulation but the weather blowing in off of Lake Michigan had been extremely cold and windy.

"Well, the ice particles on the deceased's skin had turned to a fine powder. It didn't appear to be accumulation from the hole in the roof. That leads me to believe he was in a state of extreme agitation prior to death. It was perspiration that froze on his skin. He was very much alive when he crashed through the floor, and I believe the loft above. Of course, I'm not the detective."

The sheriff nodded again, silently, biting his cheek. Often the coroner and the detective were at odds with each other. Each of them had an ego the size of Texas, and each of them wanted to show how both clever and correct he was, especially in front of the sheriff. Manny couldn't have cared less, just so they got it right.

"The autopsy confirms that both his lungs and heart showed signs of stress. There is definitely sign of myocardial infarction," the doctor said, and when he realized the sheriff was staring blankly at him, he dropped into conversational English. "He had a heart attack. But I believe it occurred after the impact with the floor. As you can see right here," the coroner said, lifting up the sheet and pointing at the deceased's waistline, "these horizontal cuts and scratches were made as he was struggling to free himself. The increased demand for oxygen, coupled with the stress, the overworked heart, the history of high blood pressure, that was more than enough to send him on his way."

Manny was glad there was someone in the world who didn't mind working with dead bodies. No matter how many years he'd serve as sheriff to the good people of Manistee County, he didn't think he'd ever get used to this part of the job.

"Then, there are the man's feet. Or the lack thereof. I'm sure you've already been prepped for this one, sheriff." The doctor fully removed the sheet, revealing the man's legs, which had been chewed off up to the ankles. They were nicely washed now, but even the sheriff could see the ragged way the skin had been torn away.

"Though I'm no expert on wildlife, I do know an animal bite when I see one. Something gnawed on the victim's feet. Judging by the lack of blood spray in the room, I would guess the feet were slowly eaten rather than being hacked off quickly. As you can see from these photos," the doctor thus handed to the sheriff, "the blood soaked into the victim's pant legs and ran down to the floor-boards. Again, I'm not the detective, but I believe the heart attack, and subsequent death, occurred just as the feet were starting to be removed."

The sheriff stood, grimly looking over the corpse before him. The coroner's report had indeed tied up all of the details involving the body and the cause of death. The detective had, without a doubt, been correct that the victim had fallen through the loft and crashed into the floorboards. But what would have prompted Dellis to climb the rickety ladder to the loft in the first place? Why was he up there?

"Of course, the most disturbing aspect was his facial appearance," the coroner finished, pulling the sheriff back from his thoughts. "He's all straightened out now, Sheriff, but you can see for yourself how he looked in the initial crime scene photos. Once we got him out of the floor, we could see his face was a frozen mask of fear. His mouth was still wide open as if he'd expelled his last icy breaths screaming for a rescue that would never make it in time before he'd frozen to death. Or before something began to take him apart a piece at a time."

* * *

The chair squeaked again as Sheriff Manny leaned over on his left elbow instead of the right. This time his left hand rubbed and massaged his forehead and temple.

The report explained the cause of death. It explained how the victim ended up stuck to his waist in the floor.

However, there were still so many unanswered questions.

The doors had been locked from within. There were no tracks, no visitors. The ladder had been pulled up into the loft, presumably before Dellis fell through the floor. What reason was there to pull the ladder up with him? Was there danger below? If so, there was no evidence of it.

The chewing of the man's feet could be attributed to wild animals. It was a harsh winter and food was scarce.

But any animals that could have gotten into the cabin and reached up three feet to eat Terry's feet, and nothing else, would still be in the cabin. There was no way to get back out except through the hole in the roof. Besides, any vermin would have stayed for the buffet until it was all gone.

And what exactly had made that hole in the roof? Could something have burst in and attacked Dellis?

The sheriff shook his head. *No*, he told himself. *You're not even going to speculate on that possibility. Next thing you know ol' Ben'll be conjuring up tales of monsters lurking in the woods. Then you'll never live that one down.*

Manny had been pouring over the report for hours, hoping that something would spark some sort of connection, but there had been none. Not one of his officers could come up with anything either.

With one last sigh, the sheriff closed the report. It was the moment that he wished he could reach over for the stamper labeled CLOSED and file the folder away for good with the others in the station's records room.

Instead, he reached out for the stamper labeled OPEN, twisting it between his fingers for a long couple of seconds.

Five minutes later, the desk lamp was switched off and Sheriff Blodgett headed home.

* * *

The news of Terry Dellis's death made the local paper, the bottom corner of the front page. But luckily the most gruesome aspects were left out. It was a short article, mostly describing the secluded life of the victim. The majority of the details were omitted, pending the ongoing investigation.

The sheriff's office was able to keep those details safe from the public for almost 40 years.

In the paper, the death was listed as probable homicide, and anyone with any leads was encouraged to contact the Manistee County Sheriff's Office. The case would be considered an open, ongoing investigation.

* * *

A week later, James Bowden awoke one dark night drenched in sweat. He sat in bed, unmoving, hardly breathing, listening intently. Then he heard it again, a long, low, lonely howl unlike anything he'd ever heard before. It only slightly resembled the howl of a wolf or coyote, only far more sinister for some reason. It had been featured in the nightmare that had awakened him so suddenly, though he'd hoped it was only a part of his imagination. But as he heard it again, he knew it wasn't just in his head. Something was lurking out in the Claybank Lake area.

It was something that didn't belong there, something not normal.

James had seen the body of his friend. Luckily for him, it was a bit too dark inside that day, compared to the brightness outside, to have completely seen the bloody stumps where Terry's feet had once been. James had pieced together enough of the officers' findings to go with the observations he'd made through the glass window in Terry's front door. He knew such an accident didn't just happen to someone. Only something truly frightening would have scared Terry into using the rickety ladder to get up into the relative safety of the loft.

But then the loft hadn't proved to be a safe spot either, had it?

And what sort of creature could have burst through the roof to get in, and then scaled its way back up, climbing out the same opening?

Maybe the same creature that's howling out there in the wild, he thought shivering.

The Tale of Sigma

The Tale of Sigma

1987

THE DIGITAL ALARM clock on the bedside table glowed a bright red 5:12 when the phone began ringing. Within a moment, a pair of skinny legs swung around the bed's edge, planting bare feet firmly on the carpeting.

Clicking the ON button, the slim man spoke into his mobile telephone, "Travis."

"You need to get yourself south right now. There's been another sighting."

"Where?" Travis said, his eyes now open widely.

"It's right in the middle of Kalkaska County. A little smudge of a town called Sigma."

Travis paused for a moment, his head matching up his knowledge of the geography of northern Michigan with the newspaper article he'd read the previous day. "You mean that forest fire this past weekend? That Sigma isn't even really a town, at least not anymore. How do you know it's a sighting?"

The contact on the phone gave an annoyed sigh. "There hasn't been anything exciting happening in your region in seven months. You really think the creature was going to take a year off?"

The government man rubbed his eyebrows with his left hand. Northern Michigan was anything but a hotbed of excitement, even in the summer. And true, there had been nothing so far this year, not even any rumors to investigate.

"It was right under your nose and you didn't notice it," the cold voice over the mobile telephone said flatly.

Travis finished yawning. "I was just going with the data we've collected. Based on the creature's movements over the past six decades, it should have been much further north. The last encounter was in Interlochen, and that's," he paused a moment, doing the math in his head, "barely 30 miles away. Each of the past decades we've tracked it, the creature has moved anywhere from 50 to 100 miles at a stretch."

"Well, you've got its location now. I don't have to tell you how urgent this whole situation has become. Don't lose track of the creature because you overestimated its range."

"Okay, I'm on my way," Travis said, quickly hanging up the phone. Within a few minutes, he was fully dressed in his non-descript navy blazer, white shirt and tie. He grabbed his travel bag, and headed out the hotel door.

* * *

His nose stung from the acrid smell of charred wood. Even the light drizzle couldn't wash away the smell. The ground was all black and shiny. The tree trunks stood like so many pencils stabbed into the earth, straight and smooth since all of the limbs and bark had been singed away.

His sedan bounced along the bumpy road. Though paved, it might as well have been a dirt road with all of the pot holes. Muddy water constantly splashed up onto the windshield, causing Travis to scowl every time he had to click the wipers on. The heavy rain might have stopped, but there was still a fine, annoying mist everywhere.

He counted a pair of county police cruisers, a red pickup with a set of emergency lights on top, and an ugly yellow station wagon.

Farther down, Travis could see a fire truck had parked at the right side of the road. *With all of this weekend's heavy rain*, he thought, *there would be no need for the fire truck.* But it was here anyway, maybe as precaution.

A collection of sheriff's deputies was standing around the bulk of a burned-out building and drinking coffee from white Styrofoam cups. Yellow caution tape had been stretched around the property from a half-dozen metal poles. A detective and the fire marshal were poking around the remains.

Locals, thought Travis. *They'll poke around a bit without any real clue what happened here.*

He parked the sedan and stepped outside. Despite the heat and humidity, Travis still wore his dark blazer. His eyes were hidden behind the aviator sunglasses. The government man stifled a groan as both shoes landed in a puddle nearly up to his ankles.

Travis looked around the area slowly as he strolled right up to the deputies. *This'll be a hard one to process*, he thought. *Between the fire and the downpour, evidence will be tough to dig up.*

But that was his job, and one way or another, he'd find something here, some clue that managed to survive the extremes of fire and water. And undoubtedly, there would be someone he could interview. Despite the remoteness of the tiny towns and villages he'd tracked the Dogman through, there was always someone with information.

"This is a crime scene, mister," the youngest of the deputies said, trying to puff up his chest and sound impressive. He'd stepped forward to intercept Travis, standing a full head taller than the government man, and now he held his big, beefy hand out in a gesture of warning. "There's an ongoing investigation here. We'll need you to head back to your car and leave the scene."

It was a situation Travis had been through many times.

"Agent Travis, NSA," the government man said, flashing his identification and security badge.

"Okay, I'm gonna need you to wait here while I check this out," the deputy said.

Travis waited patiently while the young deputy strolled around the cruiser and called in to dispatch. "Uh-huh, uh-huh, okay, okay, I uh, yes, sir, if you say so."

The government man continued to survey the scene. On the left, it appeared to be the remnants of a baseball field, though the backstop was melted and shriveled like a dead spider. There were light tendrils of smoke issuing from a huge hole in the road. On the right, the remains of buildings of some sort, but whether they had been businesses or residential structures, it was nearly impossible to make out.

"Okay, your story checks out," the deputy said loudly so his partners on the other side of the cruiser could hear. He was trying hard to save face in front of his fellow officers, seeming to give his own approval for Travis's presence in their crime scene. "You're cleared to take a look around."

But Travis wasn't done. These locals needed a lesson. It almost always came down to this, or he'd never get anything done. If he didn't establish his authority immediately, the local officers would undoubtedly get in his way and pester him during the entire investigation. He slipped his sunglasses into his breast pocket, and stared down the deputy with his cold, dark eyes, like a shark's eyes. "That's not all, is it? You were told to give me access to everything here, weren't you? And if I determine there's anything unusual, anything at all, I'm to take command of the investigation, isn't that right?" Travis said, his nearly lifeless eyes boring into the younger man.

"Um, yes, sir," the deputy muttered. The other three deputies looked on, partially fascinated that their young, beefy friend was apparently getting in over his head, and partially waiting to see what he'd do about it.

"What's your name, son?"

"Brindle, sir."

"Well, Deputy Brindle," Travis said loudly and forcefully, taking an intimidating step toward the younger, though much larger, man, "your supervisor gave you crystal clear instructions which you're to pass along to your fellow officers, didn't he?"

Brindle was now nearly at a loss of words, and had backed up a step. "Uh, y-yes, sir."

"And if you crossed me, for any reason, you'd find yourself at a new job writing parking tickets someplace in the most remote part of the U.P. known to man, right? So, do you want to tell them or should I?" Travis asked, nodding toward the cruiser and stalking yet another step closer.

Deputy Brindle quickly turned to the other officers, glad to be out of the agent's piercing stare. The other three were now sure their partner, who always claimed to them that he wasn't just the biggest and baddest thing carrying a gun, but also the youngest and best-looking man in Kalkaska County, was well over his head, and maybe they all were.

Travis wasn't interested in hearing the big man give his partners the news. It always came down to the same thing.

"Now, Deputy Brindle, why don't you get me a coffee? Black. Now."

"Um, yes, sir," the deputy said, sheepishly. His head hanging a little lower, the big deputy skittered out of the agent's way.

* * *

Agent Travis picked his way carefully around the mud puddles. They were a murky black color, thickened from the ash and debris that had floated its way to the ground. The heavy rain over the weekend had contained the fire, limiting the damage to the couple of hundred acres immediately around the remains of the village.

He'd seen untold dozens of tiny villages during his years here in northern Michigan. So many of them were the same. Or at least Sigma had once been the same.

And in this case, there was virtually nothing left of Sigma. Nothing at all. The fire marshal, who was far more cooperative than the deputies, believed that the fire was the result of an explosion of an underground gas tank. The detective confirmed the story, noting that the burned-out bulk of a building adjacent to the new hole in the earth was once a gas station, though he was pretty sure it had ceased operations several decades earlier. The tank must have been closed off and buried sometime in the past. "Yeah, the EPA would love to sink their teeth into this one, God love 'em," the fire marshal joked.

As Travis moved carefully up and down the main street he took his notes on his mobile telephone, speaking into its digital recorder. It was a very nice feature the National Security Agency had added to the communication devices utilized by all field agents. Since NSA was a subdepartment of the U.S. Department of Defense, they got all of the perks of one of the U.S. government's largest budgets. The amount of money their department had to play with in terms of just utilizing the latest in technology was more than some small countries spent in an entire year. As a result, the DoD and the NSA agents received the best and most recent advances in technology anywhere in the world. Agent Travis thought about his mobile telephone, for instance. *Civilians won't get this kind of technology for another 20 years or more. And yet, I can call any number, any place in the world. It can hold not just hours worth, but days worth of notes on its internal memory.*

Shoot, these little babies probably do more than many of the big supercomputers in Washington D.C., he thought.

He thought about giving Agent Bradley a call. Agent Bradley was the closest thing to a partner Agent Travis had. Though he was stationed in Wisconsin, tracking and studying another beast in the countryside, he often shared information with Travis. Sometimes his insight proved well to Travis's own situation. And of all the agents he'd met, Travis thought Bradley actually had a personality. He didn't mind calling up Agent Bradley to get the latest on the Wisconsin Mothman.

They often shared speculation on the purpose of their roles in the department. Obviously, someone in the U.S. government wanted tabs kept on the various monsters that were stalking the wild areas of the country. Data was collected and recorded somewhere for some purpose.

Most agents really didn't understand the bigger picture of why cryptozoology was a concern to the Department of Defense in particular. The structure of their organization was designed just so that secrecy was the top priority.

Travis and Bradley had been with the department the longest, and had even once been privy to a gathering of their bosses. It had been at a university laboratory, and a wispy-haired professor had been muddling on and on about the space-time continuum, the importance of relativity, and a whole lot more scientific jargon than Travis really cared to hear. Somehow this mad scientist was connected to the bigger picture, but Travis wasn't really impressed. He'd just as soon be out here in the field.

But at the end of it all, it was often those crazy scientific-types who provided him with a job and all of the neat tech gadgets he got to use.

Hours went by as Agent Travis slowly made his way through the remains of Sigma. He poked his way carefully around every foundation, up and down every sidewalk, and even through the wooded section that separated the village from the long field to the east. His outward façade didn't show the disappointment he felt inside. There was simply nothing to be seen here.

Yet, he could feel the Dogman's presence all around him. It was like a brief whiff of a smell he couldn't quite identify and yet knew intimately. Having tracked the beast for two decades now, Travis's gut told him it had been here. It was the cause of all of this devastation.

And the beast had gotten away cleanly, leaving no trace.

Well, Travis thought, climbing into his sedan after a long day's wasted efforts, *there might not be any physical evidence, but at least there are a few names to follow up on. Likely one of them will give me the next lead I need to catch up to the creature.*

* * *

The next day, Agent Travis had tried his best to question Eric Martin, the young DNR officer who'd apparently been on the scene when Sigma blew sky high, but the man was just too unresponsive. In intensive care, his arms were tied down across his chest to keep his broken collarbones from moving, and there were enough powerful drugs in his system to keep an addict happy for days.

Even a week later, once he had left the hospital, Officer Martin simply had no memory of the fateful night.

"Do you remember anything at all about the fire?" Travis asked gently, knowing that Martin was obviously suffering from a severe trauma. The government man had tracked Officer Martin down to his home the day he was released, eager to continue the investigation. Even after several more days of digging, there was nothing to be found in the remnants of the village. Everything had been obliterated in the fire, and the heavy rain finished the job by wiping out any actual evidence of whether the creature had been there or not.

Officer Martin had become the only link to the happenings of that fateful night, and the only link to tell if the beast had been involved.

The young man paused for a long time. His eyebrows were furrowed in deep thought as he concentrated hard. Travis gave him a lot of credit—he was giving it a really good effort.

"I'm sorry, there's just nothing there," Officer Martin said in an exasperated voice. The effort had tired him out. Travis guessed the young DNR officer was probably in his mid-20s, but there was a worn-out look to him, like he'd gone too many rounds with Mike Tyson.

"That's okay, son," Travis said soothingly, giving Martin a cold washcloth to place over his forehead. The young man smiled weakly. "Maybe, let's try something else. I have some photographs here that I'd like to show you. Maybe they might trigger something. All you have to do is look at them and let me know what comes into your mind. How would that be?"

Officer Martin thought it over for a few seconds and then tried another weak smile. "I guess we could try it."

"Take a look at this first one," Travis said, passing a Polaroid of Martin's DNR pickup. It was always easiest to begin with something familiar, and he'd taken this one in the man's driveway.

"That's my truck," Officer Martin said slowly.

Agent Travis smiled and expressed how pleased he was. "Good, good. Now, how about this one?" Again, he passed a Polaroid to the injured man.

"Sigma Corners," Martin stated flatly. His strength was beginning to wane.

Sensing that the DNR man fading, Travis cut right to the chase. "Now, have you seen anything like this before?" This time he handed over a picture of a gigantic canine-shaped footprint, pressed down into soft dirt.

As soon as the Polaroid touched Martin's fingers, the injured man's eyes shot wide open and he dropped the picture into his lap. Suddenly, Officer Martin bolted upright in his bed. A cold sweat had broken out on his forehead, and his eyes stared ahead, unblinking, either in shock or fear.

Agent Travis jerked back, instinctively, surprised by the young man's quick movement. His near catatonic state during the entire interview gave no indication that he could or would make any sudden movements.

"Officer Martin," Travis said slowly and carefully, reaching out to caress the injured man's hand gently. "Eric, can you tell me if you've ever seen that before? Can you tell me if you've seen the creature that made that footprint?"

The young man's mouth was working, his lips trying to form words, but nothing initially came out. Agent Travis leaned in closely, staring carefully at Martin's face, trying to figure out what the man was trying to say.

Two words finally came out before Martin slumped back to his bed and passed out.

Those two words were names.

The names meant nothing to Travis until he returned again to Sigma and began the arduous task of tracking down anyone who could recognize them.

Officer Martin had said, "Brian. Stevie."

* * *

"You like that ice cream?" Agent Travis asked.

"Oh, yes," Stevie said hurriedly, slurping the little streams of melted ice cream that were dripping down the cone. "Yes, sir. Chocolate is my favorite, yes, indeedy!"

Now the witness was in a great mood and the ice cream had softened their relationship. The way to a man's heart is through his stomach, Travis believed. Stevie was just like a puppy—feed him and he'd follow you anywhere. "Okay, Stevie," the agent began, "I want you to tell me about the Dogman."

Stevie stopped in mid-lick. Though his tongue was still pressed against the ice cream cone, his eyes slowly rose up to look at the agent. If Travis hadn't grown accustomed to being serious every moment of his life, he might have laughed at the comical appearance of the dim-witted boy.

Agent Travis waited. He knew that folks like Stevie here might need a little more time to process the information, a little more coaxing. In the end, all of the answers would come. But extracting the answers might take some finesse.

"You've seen it, haven't you, son?" the government man said in an off-hand way. If he threatened the boy, he'd undoubtedly clam up. It was far easier to try and keep everything light and simple and lead the boy to the right answers.

Stevie returned his gaze back to the ice cone. A few moments later, he said softly, "Yes, we seen it. In town. It was right 'fore the fire, yes, sir, it was."

"Stevie, do you know how the fire started?"

The boy stared down at his ice cream cone for a long time in what Travis guessed was deep thought. Then he started to tell the story. It came in bits and pieces, sometimes with long pauses in between. Some parts were painful for the boy to recall, and at some points he was genuinely horrified at what he remembered. But he did a fine job in the end.

Stevie and this other younger boy, Brian, had been riding with the DNR officer into Sigma the night of the fire. Some other man had been shooting a "mashing" gun, as Stevie called it, at the monster when the conservation officer's truck pulled up. Officer Martin climbed out, confronted the man. Only then did he notice the beast stand up, recovered from the dozens of bullet wounds.

Despite being told to stay put, Stevie sneaked the truck closer to the action. The unknown man then somehow shot fire from his arm, trying to burn the beast. That, as Agent Travis knew from the fire marshal's report, managed to set the underground fuel tanks on fire. The fumes and remaining fuel buried deeply underground had exploded.

Stevie could only guess the unknown man had been engulfed by the blast. However, Officer Martin was saved by the simple boy's brute strength, hauling him into the truck's cab.

The last thing Stevie remembered seeing was the dark shadow of the Dogman standing on the main street of the village, silhouetted by the intense flames behind it. In Stevie's own words, "That Dogman ain't like the werewolfs in the movies. It weren't kilt by them bullets. Not even fire hurt it. It was just like in that song, that scary song on the country channel one-oh-three point five, today's classic country favorites. That song gives me the creeps, yes, sir, it does. And it's all true!"

Travis had a feeling there was more to this simple boy. It was a hunch, and the government man had learned to trust his hunches a whole lot over the years. In his job, sometimes the hunch was all he had to go on. Sometimes the hunch could save your life.

There was something deeper, almost like an aura around the boy. It was nothing Travis could see, nothing as obvious as that. But he had a distinct feeling that, though Stevie may not be very bright, he might possess some other sort of sensory perception.

He smiled warmly at the boy. "Stevie, have you seen the Dogman before the night of the fire? Maybe someplace else?"

"Oh, yes," Stevie said, nodding his head. "That beastie was a-gonna get Brian, he's my friend, my good friend. But I saved Brian, and his girlfriend Bonnie, too. Pulled 'em right out of the cellar window, yes, I did."

"That's really great, Stevie," Agent Travis nodded, maintaining the good-cop smile. Travis didn't know what event the cellar window alluded to, but it didn't matter. This kid couldn't be pushed through anything negative; but he could be charmed. "You're a hero, you know."

Stevie blushed and gave a little shrug of his shoulders as his head drooped a little in embarrassment.

"You did real good, Stevie," Travis said approvingly. "Real good. Now, how about another ice cream cone?"

* * *

There was little else Agent Travis could do or investigate in this tiny village turned ghost town. No one was left in the area. The name "Brian" turned out to be a 10-year old boy whose family up and moved that very week without a trace. Travis had managed to interview a handful of folks who would attest to the awful howling and growling out on the Dredge at night. The Dredge, he understood, was the common name given to the large, grassy field to the east of the village. A few were still missing a family member, now presumed to be dead in the fire.

There still wasn't any evidence to report.

This wouldn't be the first time Travis had lost track of the creature. The report on Sigma wouldn't please his superiors, but they wouldn't fire him either. He'd just have to keep his eyes and ears open and be ready when the Dogman surfaced again someplace. And the creature would show up again. Without a doubt, Travis believed the Dogman was heading north. Eventually all roads heading north ended at Mackinaw City.

Why it was heading there, he only had his guesses. And there was nothing special about his guesses. They were based on experience and gut feelings that often turned out right.

That Stevie, however, Travis knew he was something special. Something a bit more than just a name in a report. Agent Travis knew he'd have to keep an eye out on that boy. It was just a hunch, but he felt that Stevie might have a larger part to play as the Dogman saga played itself out over the years to come.

Yes, he thought, climbing back into his sedan, *that kid might be useful at some point in the future. It would be a wise thing to keep track of him.* Agent Bradley had agreed when they'd talked on the phone the night before. Someone like Stevie, with a special gift, especially an extra-sensory gift of some sort, might be valuable. Very valuable, indeed.

Markus's Blog

Markus's Blog

2010

Meet the author: *Markus*

Affiliation: *former AML researcher and #1 fan*

Location: *Southern California*

Recent Post: April 7, 2008

Well hello there, to anybody out there who might take the time and energy to find me here in cyberspace, my name is Markus, and I'm a cryptozoologist.

Recent events in my life have prompted me to start up this little Dogman Blog. I don't know if I'm the only one who'll ever read it.

But either way, it's like therapy to write it all down. There's been too much, way too much, that's been filling up my mind. Worst of all, I can't hardly get the screams out of my head. It's a nightmare that just won't end at daybreak. Talk about someone who's haunted by his past!

So, anyway, I'm going to be using this blog site to try and relieve a bit of the buildup from the past few months. My therapist said it was a good idea, and maybe I can channel some of my thoughts out to folks who might be able to help me deal with what I saw, with what I experienced.

This is a free invitation —if you're reading my post, if you found your way through all the billions of web pages to my blog, please, share your stories. And if you're too afraid you think someone won't believe you, you can tell me. That's because I'm in the same boat as you. I believe because I was there, I saw it. I lived the horror.

Posted by Markus at 11:35 p.m. Click here to see all 16 comments

* * *

Recent Post: May 16, 2008

Hey, it's nice to see I'm not alone out here. My blog now has a dozen readers! Thanks guys for tuning in.

Okay, here's the story for the month. This one comes from a little town called Dansville, which is a little farming community outside of Lansing, which is Michigan's state capital for those of you who failed the sixth grade. Even if you're from way over here in California, you should still know all of the state capitals, you know.

The writer of this email says she was a little girl, maybe 9 or 10 years old, when this happened, which would have put it either in 1974 or 1975.

So anyway, she wakes up one night, really late because it's very dark out. Believe me, I know what Michigan dark is like, having spent some time in the northern part of the state. Trust me, my online friends from the metro areas, you don't know dark until you're way out in the wild. And there's plenty of wild in Michigan.

Well, she's woken up by loud shotgun blasts. She's lived on a farm all her life, so she knows the sounds that different guns make. The blasts aren't all that close, but close enough to hear. And they keep going off periodically, several blasts each minute. She can tell because of the glowing hands of the new Mickey Mouse alarm clock she just got for her birthday.

Whether it's curiosity or fear, she gets out of bed and runs to her parents' room, but they're not there. Worried now, she runs downstairs and runs right into her mother, who hugs her tightly. "What is it, Mommy?" she asks, but even then she knows there's danger, real danger. Her mother is staring out at the farmhouse front door, which is open, only the screen door keeping the late summer mosquitoes out. The little girl knows already that her daddy is out there, he's out in the midst of the shooting.

Now from down the road a bit, the two of them can see headlights. Still there's more shotgun blasts, and they're getting nearer. Her mother is frozen to the spot, unable to do any more than just hold her daughter tightly.

Then they hear some sort of ungodly howl off in the distance. It's like nothing either of them has ever heard before. It's deep, and guttural, and then another round of shotgun blasts from the back of the pickup interrupt the otherwise silent night. They're right outside the house, and the blasts echo between the house and the barn. The two girls are too afraid to move, too afraid to speak. The headlights of the truck out on the road slowly move on past their farmhouse, and still the two girls are frozen to the hallway carpet.

The minutes seem to stretch to hours as they wait.

Suddenly, the screen door jerks open, and both girls scream. But it's only Daddy. He looks tired and beat and he gives out a loud exhale of relief. Just as he leans his shotgun into the corner between the door jamb and the side wall, both mom and daughter hug him tightly.

The writer of this email tells me that she's "had recurring nightmares every night for weeks," and even after many years, she is still startled into horrific thoughts any time she hears a shotgun blast, even if it's in a movie or on TV. Her father never talked about that night, never told them what he and the neighbor men were driving away from their farms. But she has guessed. She did her research and she thinks she knows what creature was stalking the farms when she was a little girl.

My friend, I can relate, totally. The nightmares haven't stopped for me either, yet. Not a day goes by that I don't think about what happened. And I think, it's only because of my job at the time that my life was spared. My job back away from the action. Destined not to take part in the drama but to have to watch it unfold, live and uncut, before my very eyes.

Yeah, I hear you, honey. The things we live with, those things we keep locked up away in our heads, those things are awful demons, and sometimes they're based not on imagination but on real life.

Before I sign off, I want to send a shout out to my good friend Steve Nolan who's keeping the beacon lit way up there in Dogman Country. Keep it real, my friend, and thanks for the email. I know you're dealing with the same demons I am, my brother.

Posted by Markus at 11:21 p.m. Click here to see all 11 comments

* * *

Recent Post: August 21, 2008

Whoa, guys, let's tone it down a bit. It's getting a bit crazy out here.

It's me, Markus, and I do apologize to all of my good readers for the couple of posts we've gotten recently. And I'm sorry I had to turn off the Comments section. It was just getting way, way, way too much. The stories about the UFO thing, I mean, come on, I think it's just a bit obvious from the name of the blog that I'm talking about the Dogman here. For those of you just trying to ruin a good thing, man, go someplace else and bother some other folks.

So anyway, now that that's settled, I just want to remind you "normal" dudes out there that you can still send in stories, sightings, and encounters to me, but you'll just have to do it by email. It's posted at the top left column of the page. Just keep on sending them my way, and that way I can sort through the crazies and just post the stuff we all are looking for.

Okay, so, story of the month. This one was sent to me by a dude from Pinconning, Michigan. Now I had no idea where this place was, so, of course, I checked Google and now I know. East side of the state, just above the Saginaw Bay. Anyway, this guy writes that he and two friends had an encounter back in the late 1950s. He didn't give me an exact date, so naturally I can't give you one. So he says, they were heading east on Pinconning Road, and this was before the building of I-75 for all of us Gen-Xers, heading out salmon fishing on the bay. So, it's getting dark, and they got the headlights on when the van he and his buddies were in came up on something standing in the road. Well, they slowed down thinking that maybe it was a person or something, and maybe he needed help since they were really out in the middle of nowhere.

Well, they slow down to not much more than a crawl and that's when they really saw it. It was completely covered in fur with long legs and arms. And when it turned its head, the profile in the lights showed an elongated muzzle just like that of a wolf or dog. It had triangular pointed ears, that was one thing the guy really remembered. So the guy riding shotgun yells, "Go, man, go!" and they step on the gas. It just stares at them as they're passing it, and its eyes are glowing on their own, not from the van's headlights.

Of course, by this time, they're all three spooked, and they end up taking some really long way back around to get home so they're nowhere near where they saw that thing. The email said the three of them just looked at each other without speaking, trying to find any truth in each other's eyes. They finally agreed they weren't going to talk about it, not then and not ever, because that might mean it really happened.

Now here's the kicker. The last line of the email read, "I haven't told anybody that story ever since it happened, not even my family, because they'd think I was crazy."

Now, you all know I'm a skeptic at heart until I see some good evidence. But the stories, man, it's the raw feeling you get reading them that makes you wonder. Okay, so here's this old timer just spilling his guts to me. He's not looking to get rich or famous, or wind up on a TV show or the cover of Time. He's just a regular Joe. And he's telling me a story, something that's been eating him up inside for 50 years or more. I know that feeling, my friend, I know it well. One of these days, I'll share my story with you all. But not yet. I'm not sure I'm ready for that yet.

Anyway, peace out to all my good readers, and look for more from the Dogman blog as soon as I got more to tell.

Posted by Markus at 10:56 p.m. Click here to see all 18 comments

* * *

Recent Post: December 24, 2008

Hi readers, it's me, Markus, again, and I'm sending out Christmas greetings to the group. As you can see, I've turned the Comments section back on. I've come to realize it isn't fair to all of you good readers to limit you because of a few crazies out there. And honestly, it was far too much to work off of all of those emails you all have sent me. Far more work than I want, so the Comments section is back on. Please use it responsibly! By all means, please start sending in your thoughts and ideas again, because together maybe we can begin to make sense of this whole Dogman phenomenon.

This month's story comes from Ludington, Michigan. Located down the lakeshore from Traverse City, this is a resort area of beautiful beaches where gorgeous sunsets can be seen every evening.

This story is unique because it comes from a brother and sister who both emailed me sections of their story in several parts. It dates back to the mid-1980s when both were in high school. They were camping at a state forest campground adjacent to Lake Michigan. Around sunset, they had hiked to the long, sandy beach to watch the sunset with their church group friends. They walked up over the dunes and beheld the shimmering lake stretched out before them. It was breathtaking, as they remembered.

Suddenly, the younger sister pointed a ways north up the beach. Her brother at first thinks she's pointing at a large chunk of driftwood. He isn't understanding what the fuss is all about, until the dark object stands up and looks back in their direction. It wasn't a piece of driftwood, but some sort of creature that was either laying in the surf or drinking from the lake.

By this time, the entire group of teenagers, probably a dozen or so as the woman later recalled, was gawking and pointing at the creature. They could all discern its features: the long, gangly arms; the dark, furred body; the pointed snout and ears.

The sudden appearance of the group of youngsters must have startled the creature, because rather than becoming aggressive, the beast crouched in alarm, then bounded up the sand dune and out of sight into the forest beyond. The Dogman did this in only a few long leaps, the soft sand and tall, sloped dune hill not impeding it in the least.

Their emails made very clear to me that this creature leapt on two legs not four, and that its strides were very long. Both the brother and sister identified the distance from the water to the top of the dunes as about 150 feet or so. As a group, they all later tried to replicate the movement of the creature by running from the water's edge to where it disappeared from sight. Not a one of them could do it in less than a minute's time.

Posted by Markus at 5:10 p.m. Click here to see all 73 comments

* * *

Recent Post: March 8, 2009

Alright, let me please take just a minute to officially state:

PLEASE STOP SENDING ME ALL OF THE GHOST STORIES

This blog is for the discussion of the Michigan Dogman. Not that I don't like ghosts or anything. And for many years leading up to 2007, it was not only my job but my passion to look into anything and everything weird, unusual, and paranormal. But they don't interest me now. If you guys out there want to talk about ghosts, I'm sure there are dozens of blogs you can go find to do so. So please, everybody here can read the older posts, and I know you are reading them because of all the comments I get on email. You all know what we're about here, so please don't waste my time on things other than Dogman.

Thanks,
Markus

Posted by Markus at 10:38 p.m. Click here to see all 2 comments

* * *

Recent Post: June 12, 2009

Alright, here's a great story from the mid-1960s. It takes place along the Cass River between the small farm towns of Vassar and Frankenmuth. Of course the town of Frankenmuth has become rather famous as a tourist destination in the years since this event, but back at that time it was still just small town America.

Well, according to the email I received, there were a week's worth of sightings up and down the Cass River between the two towns. Residents began seeing very strange animal tracks and scratches on trees. From photos I could find online, it's not a really big river, but big enough for some small boats to cruise up and downstream. Well, folks on these boats reported multiple sightings of a two-legged creature that was stalking around the riverbank. It made big news in the two towns, which are only a few miles apart. Kids were kept home indoors, most for the remainder of the summer because parents panicked. Sheriff's posses were called out, and a curfew was enacted for the first time in either town's history.

It all brings back such vivid memories of the weeks we spent in Twin Lakes. It seems the same sorts of decisions are made by the town governments, whether the event takes place in the 1960s or the 2000s.

By the way, I also receive an email from my good friend Steve Nolan that things have pretty much returned to normal in Twin Lakes. All of the horrific excitement has calmed down finally, and it's not even brought up anymore.

Sorry, Steve, but that doesn't change the past, my man. There are far too many painful memories, and yes, I'm man enough to say fears, associated with that place. Trust me, you couldn't get me to visit northern Michigan no matter how much money you paid me.

From our research, we know the Dogman sightings occur every 10 years on the seventh year of the decade. But there have been so many other "ghostly" Dogman sightings during the in-between years that it makes me wonder, what happens to the creature the rest of the decade? If all of the sightings and encounters I've found are to be believed, the Dogman is still seen during that in-between time. The common thread I think I've discovered is that the beast is more ghostly, less "real," if that can be true. It's like it takes physical form (and aggressive and violent) only on the years ending in a "7" but in the meantime, it still can be seen.

That makes some weird sort of sense, because most of the sightings I hear about are not violent in the least. Folks encounter the beast. Both are startled. Then one of three things happens: the people run away, or the beast runs away, or maybe even both take off in opposite directions. Those stories are SO unlike the pure hostility I was witness to in 2007. And yet, these non-violent stories outnumber all others, it seems, a hundred to one.

I don't know if we'll ever know what makes the Dogman tick. Am I on to something? That's the question I leave our readers for this week. Write in and let me know what you think.

Posted by Markus at 11:19 p.m.   Click here to see all 43 comments

* * *

Recent Post: July 8, 2009

Okay, so I've heard enough about government conspiracies. As someone who has been on the inside of real paranormal and cryptozoological research, I can tell you all that these things are real. But they are of no interest to the government. There's no governmental agency that's running around collecting data on these creatures. They aren't hiding anything. They aren't protecting anything, let alone us. There's no Men In Black, that's just a movie.

And no, I don't believe the government is controlling the Dogman, letting it "loose" every 10 years to be violent. That beast is a force of nature, I mean to tell you a FORCE of nature. Or maybe a better word is unnatural. That creature doesn't belong in our world, that I can tell you from experience.

Our government has more than enough to do running itself into the ground and making us all miserable in the process. They don't need any conspiracies—they leave it to the wackos to dream that up themselves and keep themselves busy.

I say that because of a new thread of emails I've been receiving over the past few months that indicate some sort of governmental agency that's been tracking the Dogman sightings. The reports are very sketchy, but always involve straight-faced men who wear sunglasses and dark blazers and drive non-descript sedans. And they are always supposedly seen near the major Dogman sightings.

I can tell you, in my time in northern Michigan, in a true hotbed of Dogman encounters, never once did I see anybody that matched that description. Never once did any of the AML staff notice anything. And we were always on the watch, man. Reggie never left a stone unturned. He talked to everybody in every community we set up in, even the police, who mostly disdained us. If he saw somebody walking a ways off in a field or sitting nearby in a car, he'd beeline it over to him to ask questions. Believe me, if there were some governmental agent man stalking us, we'd have noticed him.

Should someone be researching the Dogman? Yeah, I think that would be good. Whether it is a natural or unnatural entity in our world, it is here, and it is here to stay. Should it be studied? I think so. The question is, whose job it would be to poke and prod around close enough to the creature to collect data on it? I know what happened the last time a scientific group tried to do just that, and the result was terrible.

Posted by Markus at 9:58 p.m. Click here to see all 26 comments

* * *

Recent Post: September 4, 2009

I say "Hang Ten" to everybody out there and welcome back to the Dogman Blog. It's me, Markus, once again shouting out to the world from here in sunny southern California. As always, I might be a ways away from all the real action, but I say thanks to all of you still kickin' it back in what I've coined "Dogman Country."

I'm in the midst of mixed emotions right now. Sure, I'm always glad to be receiving all of those stories of that infamous creature. But I'm also fighting some tears back, man. Today is the two-year anniversary of the death of my close friends and co-conspirators. It was on this date, back in 2007, when the AML team was ambushed at night near the northern Michigan town of Twin Lakes. It's time for me to come clean with you all, to share my own story. I know I've been promising it for months, and to all the loyal readers, here it finally is.

For those of you who might have been living in a cave for the past six years, America's Myths and Legends was the hottest show on cable TV. And yours truly played a leading role in the research, right from the very beginning. We had some of the best tools, the best technology available to any mobile scientific lab. We had a great team. And we had a great leader, Reggie Bushman, a man amongst boys on the cable lineup each week. Can you dig it?

I tip my hat to you, Reggie. You are missed by millions of fans. And even though we worked together, I was always, and still remain, your number one fan.

We were the top show each week, with over 29 million households tuning in. Reggie was a showman, a real gem. And our entire staff nailed the footage each week. Our research was right on for each season.

And then, the fateful summer of 2007 brought us to northern Michigan. The Dogman was second only to tracking Bigfoot for Reggie. And trust me, I was there when he did shoot the Bigfoot with the tracking device. It just was an inferior design and it didn't hold. But I can tell you that Bigfoot is real, just as the Dogman is real. Our show was no hoax, man. It was the real deal.

So anyway, we'd been tracking the Dogman for weeks, and finally identified its lair. Well, Reggie sets up the season finale to broadcast right from the catacombs where the beast was living. It was going to be a beautiful thing—there were cameras and microphones mounted all over to capture the greatest footage in the history of cryptozoology.

And then the beast returned far earlier than expected. It had somehow shaken loose Reggie's GPS tracking device and trapped the AML field crew in the tunnels. It was fortunate enough that it was too dark for the cameras to send back any images. The screams and cries for help coming through loud and clear over the microphones were enough to give us plenty of mental images, those that are with us for life.

The entire field crew was decimated. And those couple of us at the communications center had to bear witness to the whole thing. There was nothing we could do to help, only listen to the sounds of those men's deaths and the cold brutality of the Dogman.

A lot of people thought our show was a fake, just a show to boost ratings on an otherwise mediocre cable channel. But I can tell you, it was real. It was all real. And the ending of the show, the story no one ever got to tell the public, the story I just wrote here was real, too.

It hurts just remembering it, but it does feel better to share the story, the story no one has ever heard before. The TV execs tried to get us to sign waivers of confidentiality, they threatened to sue us, but I never did sign. The world at large may not ever find out what happened, but those of you here on the Dogman blog now know the truth.

Posted by Markus at 12:04 a.m. Click here to see all 64 comments

* * *

Recent post: January 5, 2010

Okay, folks, here's my first entry for the month. Another year has started, and still the stories of the Dogman keep surfacing. In this post, I'd like to take a few lines and give my two cents on that Gable Film that we've all been watching so closely online. I know folks are watching it because of all the hits it's been getting on YouTube.

You know, this was one of the first bits of amateur evidence I've seen that looks the closest to the real thing. I mean, you all know that we've seen dozens of photos from all over, and especially in Michigan and Wisconsin. And I'll be honest, I gotta say quite a few of them are bogus. I mean it, man. Something fuzzy in the corner of the photo? It's a trick of the light and the shadows, nothing else. Something blurry running past the film? No way. As someone who's seen the beast up close and personal, I'm here to tell you all these pranksters don't even come close.

Of course there are a couple of photos that make me wonder. But I got to say, if you've been close enough to the beast to actually get a photo, I am truly amazed you've lived to tell the tale. Because I can say, from personal experience, that there's no stopping that thing.

Now that Gable Film, that truly brings back nightmares. It gives me the shakes just watching it. Sure it's grainy and blurry. But I can honestly say that's the closest thing to the real thing I've ever seen. And I watch all of the Hollywood renditions of werewolves. Whether its masks or makeup or CGI, they don't even come close to the real thing.

But that Gable Film, that's the real deal. According to the story that accompanies the video, and believe me, I've picked up my own copy of that CD/DVD set from that radio station in Michigan. It's not for me to give away free advertising here on the blog, but if you email me, I can send you the website to order it from. Anyway, the story states that the video was found at an estate sale, that the film was almost wrecked from years of exposure outdoors, and that the identities of the people in the video are unknown. We don't know who they were, where the film was shot, or what happened to them. Of course from watching the video, we know the beast attacked the camera man and the final shot is from the perspective of looking through the grass at ground level, where the camera fell.

As one who has seen the Dogman for real, I can tell you that the beast in the film not only looks the part but it moves the exact same way as what I've seen with my own eyes. And I've seen it both on two legs and on four. Believe me, we had the video evidence. Well, we HAD it, up until the TV execs took everything away. Everything down to the paperclips was taken. I couldn't tell you if it was destroyed or stored away in some secret warehouse in Iowa. It's gone, probably for good, never to be seen by the eyes of the world. And really, after the horror of the AML season finale, there was no way the world could see what really happened. You think the TV execs had a hard enough time trying to explain why the series was so suddenly cut short? Imagine if they'd run the footage and then tried to explain it was real and not fiction. Or fiction and not real. Or any explanation of any sort.

Now, enter the second piece of matching evidence. It's called Gable Film 2, and you can find it on YouTube, too. In this video we have documented footage from a police investigation, and the victim looks exactly like the person from the first Gable Film, right down to the hair and clothing. And the victim is an awful bloody mess, exactly what you'd expect from a Dogman attack.

These two videos have nothing in common in terms of who posted them or where they came from. Is it just possible that there is a connection between them? Did someone make the connection after seeing the first Gable Film? Or is it just a coincidence?

I've got to believe there's more to these Gable Films. Unfortunately, no one has come forth with any explanations. If anybody out there can give me something, anything, to check on, I'll be happy to research it. I've got time on my hands, that's for sure.

Here's what I do know. The Dogman is for real. And the ending of that Gable Film is exactly the type of ending for anybody who gets that close to the beast.

Posted by Markus at 10:37 p.m. Click here to see all 22 comments

The Tale of Foster City

The Tale of Foster City

2017

THE SNOWSTORM CONTINUED to ravage the countryside. The heavy white curtain of snow had been falling for a week. It paused for only a bleak, gray hour in the afternoon before redoubling its efforts.

At that point in the storm's lull, Don Staniway quickly took advantage of the situation and plowed his way through the foot and a half of snow to the woodshed out back. The trip might have been only 30 feet, but it was an excursion that mostly wore him out. Don had the little aluminum snow shovel (with the customary bent corners from years past) available to him, but by the time he would have finished a path, the chore of restocking the cabin's firewood supply was completed. Sure his feet and legs were sore (and the lower third of his jeans were soaking wet, as well as his socks despite the heavy Sorrels he wore), but the task had been completed. There would be heat in the cabin for a few more days.

Still a week before Thanksgiving, and already Old Man Winter's settled himself in for the long haul, Don thought as he stoked up the fire. He'd slipped on a new double pair of wool socks and hung the wet ones on a nail behind the old cast iron wood stove.

It was an old cabin, originally a hunter's cabin, and Don had heard it went back in the Turner family as far as the early 1900s. Though basic indoor plumbing and electricity had been run to the cabin back in the 1950s, there were very few comforts of home to be found. A pair of mismatched garage-sale lamps provided the only light inside the two room cabin. The small bedroom, just a corner walled-in as an afterthought, had no light at all, only a window. There was no TV, and Don was stuck with an old FM radio that spat more static than stations.

Someone had added a thin layer of insulation beneath a second layer of exterior siding, but it was still cold inside, especially in the Upper Peninsula winters. To keep out the cold drafts that managed to find their way through, Don had nailed thick, woolen blankets up against the walls. He even covered all of the windows except the one above the kitchen sink. Just like the thick tapestries in a medieval castle, the hanging blankets made it at least tolerable inside the cabin. However, Don still dressed in layers. It was always easier to take a layer off than to shiver while adding on more clothes.

That, of course, was the problem with the cabin. It was either too blasted hot near the wood stove or too chilly near the outer walls. The only good spot was situated right at the point where the intense heat met the cool air, and that was where Don had set his easy chair and a square card table. To pass the time, Don played solitaire. A lonely man's game, his father always called it. Well, he was a lonely man in a lonely place.

Situated right in the corner of Dickinson County, only a few hundred yards from where Marquette County and Menominee County met, the Turner cabin was indeed in the middle of nowhere. And in the winter, there were fewer folks out in the middle of nowhere.

It might be 2017, but Michigan's economy was only finally starting to recover, and a job was a job. Don hadn't held down a regular job since the depression of 2009. But he was a jack-of-all-trades and made himself available for all sorts of handyman jobs on the outskirts of Dickinson County. The Turner family trust was paying him a very nice sum to babysit this little hobby horse farm. All he had to do was keep himself and the horses out in the barn alive and well until the first of April. *Well, keeping the horses alive anyway,* the caretaker thought to himself, even though Anthony, the Turner's steward, had paid him a third up front, just enough to stock the cupboards and the old Frigidaire. The balance would be paid to him at the end of the job.

Don's rusty old Ford pickup wouldn't have much trouble in the snow, but every trip into town burned far more gas than he had money to refill the tank. He had an extremely accurate count of the money he'd been paid and the amount he'd still need to make it until April. He didn't want to run out of food before the job was done. It was just easier and cheaper to just stay put.

Really, there wasn't much that Don needed. A couple of cases of Old Style beer, a big box of frozen pasties that the local North Dickinson school kids were selling as a fundraiser, and a few pounds each of potatoes, onions, and bacon made up his meals on most days. A tall-sided cast iron fry pan and matching lid cooked up his meals right atop the wood stove. Sure, he'd love some smoked fish, but the trip to Escanaba wasn't worth the gas.

Little things like eggs, bread, cheese curds, and ketchup ran out much quicker. He didn't worry about butter since he had loads of bacon fat. So about every two weeks, he'd fire up the old Ford and take a drive into Hermansville to the IGA, or to Ebeling's Grocery in Norway. The distance was about the same whether he went west or east once he got to US-2.

The Turners were undoubtedly wintering in some warm climate. There was plenty of money in the Turner family, more than enough to have their horses sheltered in some pampered, country-club type of setting.

However, the part of the family that currently controlled the family fortune wasn't much into horses. They certainly never rode them. Don had been doing handiwork on this little ranch for years and the only person he met there was Anthony, the steward, a stocky, slightly graying fellow who lacked anything resembling a personality. Even Anthony didn't like to spend much time up here in the hills, preferring instead to manage the family's luxurious lakeside villa. But the Turners owned hundreds of acres of property all over the county and Anthony's job was to keep it all in order and make it presentable when any members of the family did venture into northern Michigan.

Don didn't much care for the steward. He seemed standoffish and snobby. But Anthony always paid in cash.

The beasts in the stable were only a step or two above wild. Oftentimes they would stamp their feet or even nip at Don when he was cleaning their stalls, especially lately, when the storm had kept them from exercising out in their pen. They were beautiful animals, that was for sure, but they were downright mean when they didn't get their way.

The daylight had nearly faded and shadows had crept up on the violet-gray world. The two little lamps cast their golden glow upon the two sides of the cabin's large central room. Suddenly, the wind died down and the inside of the cabin was eerily silent. It was the first time in over an hour that the gale wasn't blasting into the wooden siding.

The horses were raising an awful ruckus now, loud enough to be heard across the snow-covered yard. Don gave a few moments of thought to checking on them, but in a few seconds, the whinnying was drowned out by the storm once again. Don shrugged and then returned his attention back to the cards. Nine of clubs…Queen of spades…Six of clubs. Don's gnarled fingers slid the Six up into place over the Seven of hearts.

And then a chill ran down his spine, and the hairs on the back of his neck prickled up. Something didn't feel right to the old caretaker.

He looked up at the cabin's only uncovered window, and his mouth went dry. The color went out of his face. He was absolutely frozen to the easy chair.

There was something looking back in at him.

Nobody in his right mind would be out in this storm. Nobody in his right mind would be way out here in the first place. The nearest neighbor was over six miles away, and the closest town, Felch, was another dozen miles after that. Foster City was really closer, but its name was truly an oxymoron. A couple of houses and a bed and breakfast really didn't make it a city. Foster City was really more of a road bump; it didn't even qualify as a village. There might be some crazy folks living way out in the sticks here in the U.P., but not a one of them would be crazy enough to be out in a storm like this.

But it really wasn't the face of a person looking back in at him.

Even in the near darkness Don could tell the face was more of an animal than a human. The face elongated to a pointed snout, like that of a wolf or a huge dog, and Don was sure he could just make out tall, triangular ears back above the black, wispy fur. Some of the long hairs that weren't frozen in place wriggled in the wind.

Petrified in his ratty easy chair, the caretaker gripped the arms tightly. He didn't move, he didn't blink. He didn't even breathe. Every second seemed an eternity as the horrible visage stared into the cabin with its glowing yellow eyes.

But when Don thought he'd seen the worst, the face turned its lips up in what he could only think of as an awful smile. Long, sharp teeth were revealed, slightly glowing from the cabin's inside light.

And then suddenly the entire cabin shook violently, though Don couldn't tell if it was a tremendous gust of wind or if it was caused by the creature looking back in at him.

The lights went out, and Don screamed.

* * *

The next morning, the storm had passed, though the steel gray clouds still covered the sky.

Don awoke, shivering, beneath the small square table. His head hurt tremendously, and only after he rubbed his temple with his left hand, feeling a knotty bump, did he remember what happened the previous night.

Slowly, he tried to piece together the events as best as he could remember them.

The power had been knocked out.

He'd tripped in the dark and bashed his head on the edge of the table.

He could see his breath this morning because the fire had gone out.

The fire had gone out because he hadn't refilled the wood stove.

It was fairly dark now because there still was no electricity.

The power had been knocked out by...the storm?

That would be the easiest explanation, the safest explanation, the most rational explanation. Because the other explanation defied rational thought.

Kneeling, one arm on the card table, Don stopped himself. His head slowly turned to face the window. Only blank gray light poured in this morning.

Nothing there looking in at him, just as he knew there wouldn't be. And yet, Don had to know for sure. He had to check.

Head now pounding, the old man staggered his way to the door. He grabbed his barn jacket from the hook and slipped his feet into his Sorrels.

It had to have been his imagination. Indigestion caused by overly greasy fried potatoes. The power had gone out in the storm, he'd hit his head, and this combination had given him one spook of a realistic nightmare.

The heavy snow had piled up against the outside walls of the cabin. There was probably eight inches of snow that had fallen, and the high winds had blown everything level. It was as if the entire world was covered with one smooth layer of Cool Whip.

There were no definitive tracks that he could see. However, as he rounded the northwest corner of the cabin, Don's breath caught in his throat.

The drifting snow hadn't quite erased the trail that led from the woods 200 yards away right up to the cabin's north wall and right up to the only window that wasn't covered up with thick woolen blankets.

The trail wasn't fresh, there were no tracks to be seen, and it had nearly been filled back in with the drifting snow. But the trail was there, there was no doubt about it.

Don was positive that something had come right up to the cabin. It had looked right in the window at him. And at some point after the power went out, the "thing" had wondered its way back out to the forest.

It couldn't have been a person.

Don turned back to the cabin, following the trail right up to the siding. His eyes moved from the snowy ground up to the small window. The sill was right at eye level, set high for clearance over the kitchen sink, the rough backsplash and the knife rack on the other side of the wall.

Don knew he was about six feet tall, a couple of inches more with his heavy boots and standing on a bit of packed snow. A moment of calculation told him all he needed to know. Whatever had been looking in at him stood seven feet or taller.

A chill ran through his body, and it wasn't from the cold weather. He'd walked outside trying desperately to convince himself that the episode from the previous night was just a nightmare.

But it hadn't been his imagination after all. Something real had been here. Something huge, something sinister. Something that his mind told him was a beast that walked like a man.

About the author:

WITH AN ENGLISH degree from Michigan State University and a master's in educational leadership from Central Michigan University, Frank Holes, Jr. is a teacher of literature, writing, and mythology at the middle school level and was recently named a regional teacher of the year. He lives in northern Michigan with his wife Michele, son James, and daughter Sarah.

All three of Frank's Dogman books have seen tremendous success in and around the Great Lakes region. And both novels in his children's fantasy series, <u>The Longquist Adventures</u>, have been a hit with elementary students through adults.

See all of Frank's novels on his website:

http://www.mythmichigan.com

About the cover artist & illustrator:

CRAIG TOLLENAAR LIVES in southwest Michigan with his wife Traci and his daughters Isobel and Stella, and a peculiarly skinny dog named Ruby. He earned a Bachelor of Arts from Alma College and has been working as a creative artist of some sort for some time.

He spends much of his day with any type of instrument that makes a mark on a page. He enjoys living in the Midwest (and its meteorological uncertainties) and an occasional good time. Craig's impressive artwork can also be seen on the cover of *Year of the Dogman*, *The Haunting of Sigma*, *Nagual: Dawn of the Dogmen*, as well as the cover and interior pictures in both novels *Western Odyssey* and *Viking Treasure* in the series *The Longquist Adventures*.

Stop by and visit Craig's webpage:

http://www.cjtcreative.com

About the editor:

ANIEL A. VAN Beek believes that grammar is an art form and punctuation a puzzle to be solved. He is the author of one book and has also served as editor on many others, including the latest Dogman and Longquist books. Daniel is a graduate of the University of Michigan and continues to hold out hope that his beloved gridiron Wolverines will reclaim their former glory. While but a craftsman of words, he enjoys the work of those who create in any medium, from paint to music, to beer. Daniel lives in southwest Michigan with his wife, Jennifer, his son Ezra, and his daughter Lois.

8096564R0

Made in the USA
Charleston, SC
07 May 2011